LAKE HONOR

BOOGER MCCLAIN OZARKS DETECTIVE SERIES BOOK 2

ALAN BROWN

BRIAN BROWN

World Castle Publishing, LLC
Pensacola, Florida
Copyright © Alan Brown & Brian Brown 2023
Hardback ISBN: 9798387291456
Paperback ISBN: 9781960076465
eBook ISBN: 9781960076472
First Edition World Castle Publishing, LLC, April 3, 2023
http://www.worldcastlepublishing.com

Cover: Karen Fuller
Editor: Karen Fuller

CHAPTER 1
REFLECTIONS

Branson was nothing like I remembered. I had not been to the small, picturesque southwest Missouri town in over forty years. The Dairy Queen and the one-chair barbershop, the café and dime store I knew were now memories of days passed. Branson was a town on steroids. The downtown I visited in my youth had been replaced with a boardwalk and retail district dubbed Branson Landing, which lined the shores of Lake Taneycomo. Crowds of people roamed the dozens of shops and restaurants, where I recalled a quaint park overlooking the calm waters of a largely uncommercialized, uncorrupted lake.

The innocence of the small town I remembered had been replaced by neon signs, casual and fine dining, souvenir shops, a scenic railway, a twelve-story convention center and hordes of visitors. Branson resembled a smaller version of Las Vegas. It seemed odd to me that everything could change so much. Branson was transformed. It was a bona fide tourist attraction. It seemed it had sold its very soul.

There are memories in everyone's life that are unforgettable: graduation, marriage, a child's birth, and the deaths of the ones you love. Time has a way of enhancing the good memories and softening the bad ones. But there are other memories that never change, memories that seem to be frozen in time, such as the ones I had of Branson and the nearby School of the Ozarks.

They weren't all fond memories, but they weren't exactly bad memories, either. They were the kind that found their way back into my dreams and nightmares time and again over the years. That's what brought me back more than four decades later.

I wanted to bring closure to the ghosts of my past. Branson was the first stop. The destination was College of the Ozarks, just south of the supercharged small town. I had been a student there in the summer of 1973. Back then, it was called School of the Ozarks. Most students just called it S of O. For me, it was a time of innocence and naivety. It was a time of coming of age, of learning to be independent.

School of the Ozarks was not my first choice, second, or even in the top ten schools I wanted to attend. I had counted on getting an athletic scholarship to Kansas, Missouri or perhaps Bowling Green. But a serious health problem and a three-week hospital stay my senior year ended those hopes.

My family wasn't poor, but they weren't well-off either. They certainly couldn't afford to send me to college.

It was my older half-brother that told me about School of the Ozarks. He grew up in Branson. A star athlete in baseball and football at Branson High, he received a scholarship to Southwest Missouri State, now called Missouri State. He played baseball one season and was drafted by the Seattle Pilots, now called the Mariners. He never made it past single-A ball. An arm injury cut his career short, and he went on to barber college, eventually going to work in a small barbershop in downtown Branson.

That shop is gone now, swallowed up by progress. So is Ron. He passed away a few years ago, but his heart and soul never left Branson. He was a wonderful man, caring, loving, gentle, a kind soul, just like the town he loved so much and the people that lived there.

Ron paved the way for my visit to the school. He talked to the track and cross-country coach. He talked to people in the administration he knew. S of O was a small, private school with less than eight hundred students. A lot of people knew Ron. He came to campus twice a week and cut hair for the students. He had made a lot of friends.

School of the Ozarks was a prayer answered for me.

It was a free college. Everyone who attended worked on campus to earn their education. I had no idea a place like it existed. And as you can imagine, the opportunity to get a free college education was extremely popular. Only a small percentage of students who applied to S of O were accepted. The administration could pick and choose their student body.

When I visited, everything was set, with no lengthy vetting process. All I had to do was apply. I was admitted to the school that summer semester. The student selection process was generally long and intensive. The school considered financial need, dedication to Christian values and academic performance. Then they considered how a student would fit into their culture. It was extremely conservative. Rules were strict, and punishment for breaking those rules was even stricter.

They believed in building Christian values and a strong work ethic. A large, white stone chapel named the Williams Memorial Chapel was the centerpiece of the campus. I remember attending services there every Wednesday evening and every Sunday morning. It was mandatory. "Strengthen the soul, and the mind and heart will follow," I remember someone telling me.

Like many new freshmen, I pushed the envelope as far as I could when it came to "conforming" to the rules. As a child of the 60s, the rule about hair length was one of my biggest issues. Men's hair was not to hang more than one-quarter of the way past the top of the ear lobe. I had always worn long hair in high school. Cutting it was painful. I constantly combed it behind the ear and toward the back but on windy days, and there were a lot of them, my hair had a mind of its own. I received several warnings about my hair.

The nightly curfews were also a problem for me. We were required to be in our dormitory by 10 p.m. on weeknights and midnight on weekends. At eighteen, I was enjoying my first taste of freedom. The curfew was a difficult pill to swallow. With time, I found ways around the restriction: sneaking out through my window, saying that I was going home for the weekend, and simply not coming back until the dormitory doors were unlocked early the next morning. Breaking the rules came with a risk of expulsion, and thinking back on it now, I can't believe I took those risks.

Most of the student body came from small towns, many from the surrounding Ozarks communities. These were genuinely good people. They worked hard. They didn't ask for a lot out of life. Serving God, making friends and taking care of family seemed to be most students' main concerns. The pace was slow. Days were long. Work was hard. But they relished life.

The friendships I made represent some of the fondest memories I have.

North of the school, but south of Branson, is the town of Hollister. Just a couple of miles southwest of Hollister is the entrance to School of the Ozarks. When I entered the campus coming off the two-lane highway, I was amazed at how little things had changed. It looked as if the school had been frozen in time. It was exactly the way I remembered it.

No more than a ten-minute drive from an area completely transformed, the school looked like it had been untouched by progress. The large, gray-stoned buildings that dotted the campus were still there. They looked to be nearly a century old. But age had not changed them. They looked exactly as they did four decades earlier.

The gravel road leading from the entrance gate to the campus was just like I remembered. A gravel road that tossed up dust and rocks under the weight of car tires. The large stone church was just to the west of the road, near the center of the campus. The cafeteria, the Fine Arts building, and the church all looked exactly the way I remembered them.

The science building, new in 1973 and the only building with a touch of modern architecture, was still there. Oddly, it was the only building that appeared to age with time.

There were a few changes, of course. The athletic building appeared to be new. That was a good thing. The one I remembered was old. Plaster was crumbling in the locker rooms. The concrete floor in the weight room and basement was uneven and buckling in a few spots. The ceiling leaked during heavy rains, and the temperature inside was either too hot or too cold. I remember birds used to fly around in the rafters of the old gym. The large indoor swimming pool in a separate section of the athletic building was in serious need of repair. It reminded me of the high school pool in the movie "*It's a Wonderful Life.*" It was dark, musty and cold.

The cinder, oval track I used to work out on was gone too, replaced by a rubber track, six lanes across with bleachers on either side. I remember how that old track was uneven, worn down by cleats that were necessary to gain any traction on it during rainy days. Six laps to the mile. It wasn't a regulation track. We couldn't host any track events on it. It was strictly used for practice.

The dormitories were just as I had remembered, too. Three dorms, two for men and one for women. The newest of the men's dorms had been built only a few years before I attended school there. It had air conditioning, the only one of the three dorms that did. It was used to house upperclassmen, juniors and seniors.

I was housed in the old dormitory. For an eighteen-year-old away from home for the first time, it was a scary place. It was dark, cold in the winter and hot in the summer. The floors were an ugly fading green linoleum, yellowed with age. The paint on the walls was peeling. The rooms were small, smaller than my bedroom at home. Lined down a long, narrow hallway, each room was identical. A large communal bathroom and shower were located on each floor.

When I first saw the inside of my dormitory, I thought

it looked like something I would imagine of an old psychiatric hospital in a horror movie. In fact, when I first watched the movie "*Halloween*," and saw the mental hospital where Jason escaped, I immediately thought about that dorm.

But, mostly, I was glad to see much hadn't changed. The stone walkways that led students from building to building were still there. The old black lamp posts that dotted campus were exactly as I remembered. They were always so warm and inviting, particularly on a cold winter's night when the snow was falling, and the smell of hot chocolate and freshly made smores engulfed the air around the fire pit on the shores of Lake Honor.

The lake was the reason I had come back. It had become a part of me in the short time I was there.

If there were two iconic landmarks on campus that, more than anything, represented to me the soul of the school, those would be the Williams Memorial Chapel, aka Stone Chapel, and Lake Honor. They were the constants that would never change. They were the places people went to celebrate life and the places people went to hide their darkest secrets.

Lake Honor was not really a lake. It was more like a pond, circular, less than an acre in size and man-made. It was a place of reflection, a place where young love blossomed and a place where the troubled and tired could reminisce about their carefree days. For the most part, it was a happy place.

I have a lot of fond memories of Lake Honor. I fell in

love for the first time on a bench under the shadows of the sprays of water that jetted up from the fountain at the lake's center. I came there when I was lonely, scared or just wanted to be alone with my thoughts.

Lake Honor was beautiful. It judged no one. It was a warm place on a cold, lonely night. The gentle ripples in the water and the relaxing sound of the water from the fountain lifting high in the air and arcing back into the lake like the gentle touch of a mother lying her baby down in the crib for a night's sleep. I spent the best of times and the worst of times at Lake Honor.

It was the last place I visited when I returned to campus some forty-four years after I left. I took a seat at the same bench where I'd sat many times before. It was warm now, late summer. The trees were green. The air was dry when I arrived, and the wind was still. The lake had a quiet elegance. It was calm and peaceful.

When I first arrived on campus, I thought Lake Honor seemed to have an innocence about it. Its simple fountain in the middle reminded me of home. Kansas City has a lot of fountains. It reminded me of my childhood. I was naïve back then, full of hope, full of optimism. I was ready to embrace life.

For me, it always felt like more than a lake. Even today, I can feel its pull on my soul. It's like a magnet drawing me closer to answers, to resolution, to rest. It's a transcendent place where roads begin and end.

I went there often during the two semesters I spent at S of O, mostly late at night after curfew when it was quiet, and the only noise you could hear was the sound of ripples created by the fountain.

Life at S of O was not easy for me. Beyond the shores of the tiny, man-made lake, I never felt I belonged. I could never be fully comfortable there. I had friends, good friends, and for the most part, my memories of S of O were good. But I was always anxious to leave. From the first day I walked onto campus, I knew I would not be a student there very long. The strict rules, the curfews, and the requirement to attend church twice a week and take certain religious courses did not sit well with me.

The funny thing was that I had grown up in a strong Lutheran family. I had attended church services most Wednesday nights and Sunday mornings ever since I could remember. But before, it was my choice. No one told me I had to attend church. No one forced me to do it. No one threatened me with punishment if I chose not to go. My parents had always trusted me to do the right thing. If I wanted to miss a church service now and then, they would understand. They never punished me for missing.

But it was different at S of O. They used rules, punishment and threats to force conformity. At least, that was how I saw it, and I did not handle rules well, particularly those I didn't understand. That large, white stone church in the center of campus became a thorn in my foot, a thorn that I was determined to get out. For my first few weeks, I attended church as I was required. But I watched and looked for any opportunity to bend the rules. I soon found my chance with an attendance card that was handed out when you walked into church. The card would be completed, and then when the service was over, the card would be put into a locked box as the student left the church.

So, I would come to church early, fill out the attendance card, drop it in the outgoing box, and leave. In hindsight, it was a stupid plan. Had anyone checked the locked box before the service ended, they would have seen the lone attendance card inside, and that would have likely gotten me expelled. But I was lucky. No one checked, and I continued to do the same routine every Wednesday night and Sunday morning.

I avoided that church nearly my entire time at S of O.

Lake Honor was my church. Its shores were my alter. It offered the spiritual guidance I refused to accept from the strict Stone Chapel. Whenever I felt lost or needed answers, I went to Lake Honor.

I felt the lake nourished my soul and protected my innocence until the pivotal day when everything changed.

It was the fall of '73. The air was crisp. The leaves on the trees were no longer green. They had changed to their autumn colors, orange, brown, and red. The trees were breathtaking that time of year. The Ozarks in the fall was a magical place. I can't imagine anything more beautiful. The colors were spectacular. The air was fresh. The quiet was deafening. It was a place where you could hear individual leaves fall. Where the rush of modern life felt a million miles away.

The night before everything changed for good had been a stormy one with bright lightning flashes and booming thunder. Lights in the dormitory flickered on and off but never totally lost power. The wind was strong, blowing branches against the windows and making a terrible clatter.

The storm seemed to come out of nowhere. The weather could change on a dime in the Ozarks. It had been sunny and unseasonably warm earlier in the day. Clouds had begun to roll in during the early evening. By 10 p.m., the wind was howling. The temperature had dropped, and the rain had begun to pour.

It was difficult to sleep that night. Growing up in Kansas, I had seen storms like this come on rapidly from the west. Sometimes they produced the tornadoes for which Kansas was famous. I remember being concerned a tornado might come that night. The storm was eerily similar to one I remembered that spun several tornadoes and destroyed a large portion of Topeka in the late '60s.

For nearly two hours, the driving rain pelted the small college on the hill. Then it disappeared from Point Lookout as quickly as it came.

When I woke a few hours later, a fog had blanketed the campus. It wasn't surprising. The temperatures had changed rapidly from warm to cold to warm again as the storm passed through. With the Branson area nestled around three lakes, S of O often experienced fog from the lakes in the valley below when temperatures changed rapidly.

Usually, the fog appeared during the early morning hours and disappeared by mid-morning. That was the case that day. It was heaviest on the way to my first class. By the time I came outside again, it was gone, replaced by clear blue skies.

The day would not have been remarkable had it not been for what the storm brought with it. I remember very little about it at all until a little past 1 p.m. I had a Religion class from noon to 1:00 that day, and the cafeteria stopped serving lunch at 1:30 p.m., so I rushed from the fine arts building, planning to eat at the cafeteria about a hundred yards away. I was very hungry. I had skipped breakfast earlier in order to sleep in a little.

I didn't make it to lunch, though. I was distracted by a loud sound, like a motor grinding, coming from Lake Honor, about fifty yards away. To this day, I don't remember why I decided to check it out instead of going to eat. Curiosity, I guess.

A few steps toward the lake, the sound stopped, and

along with it, the fountain.

I remember thinking that maybe the power had shut off or that tree limbs and debris from the storm the night before might have fallen into the water and clogged the fountain's motor. Or, it could have just been routine maintenance. But I noticed there weren't any workers around.

As I got closer to the lake, I saw two items float to the surface. At first, I thought it was debris, maybe two large branches from one of the massive oak trees. I was near the shore's edge when I realized what I was looking at. I couldn't believe it. Two bodies, fully clothed, were floating on the lake's surface.

The sight of those two boys floating on top of the water haunts me still, transforming dreams into nightmares. For me, the innocence of S of O was lost that day.

Shortly after the bodies were discovered, it was announced that neither of the boys were students at the school. Soon after, it was determined they died from drowning. Their deaths were ruled accidental.

But most students, it seemed, couldn't believe what they were told. I, for one, had difficulty understanding how two boys with no connection to the school would wander onto the campus late at night and go swimming in the lake fully clothed.

"They were drunk, maybe on drugs." I remembered one student had said, attempting to validate the coroner's report.

"But how did they get sucked down to the bottom of the lake?" another student asked.

"They probably got too close to the fountain and got sucked under," someone replied.

The fact was that non-students rarely got on to campus, particularly late at night when the gates were shut. In my mind, it just didn't make sense. It was certainly possible they got past the gates, onto campus, avoided security and jumped into Lake Honor fully clothed. But why?

Branson was surrounded by three large lakes. If a person had the desire to jump in the water fully clothed, why not choose nearby Table Rock or Taneycomo? Lake Honor was small. It was in the middle of campus. Student housing was a short distance away. Campus security patrolled the area.

It was not a crime to swim in one of the three lakes, even fully clothed. But coming onto a private campus after curfew could have gotten them in a lot of trouble. I was convinced whatever happened to those young men was no accident.

Like one falling leaf after another, my life soon changed dramatically. My dad passed away two weeks later. He was only forty-one years old. A massive heart attack took him. My mother called to tell me the news. I spent the following two weeks at home with my family. After returning to S of O, I was a different person, less naïve, more cynical and more anxious to live life. I had never remembered my dad being sick, not a cold or the flu. I don't think he ever missed a day of work. When he died, I realized that life could end abruptly at any time. I was determined to live mine to the fullest every day and not to take tomorrow as a given. I was no longer a conformist. I partied almost every night. I stopped paying attention to curfews or rules of any type. I did what I wanted to do and when I wanted to do it.

I understood why God took my father. But I didn't have an answer for what happened to those boys. And memories of that day are never far away. I was a journalism major at that time. My heroes at the time were Carl Bernstein and Bob Woodward, who investigated the Watergate conspiracy. I could not think of a more noble profession than to be an investigative reporter. I aspired to be like my heroes. I had to make sense of this. No longer innocent, seeing the world for what it was, I had to investigate the deaths of the boys found dead at my altar.

My stay at S of O would be short-lived. I'd move on to a different college after the Fall semester. The rebel that had taken over my personality would soften with time. But the memory of those two boys floating in Lake Honor refused to go away. They, like my father, represented the fragility of life.

CHAPTER 2
NEAR AND FAR

Steve Raymond and Gary Walker grew up less than twenty miles apart. Gary was born and raised in Nixa, MO., a little town of around ten thousand just a few minute's drive south of Springfield. Steve lived in Springfield, the third-largest city in the state. They came from different social classes, and their paths would have likely never crossed if it wasn't for their choice of vocation after high school. Both wanted to learn woodworking. They wanted to become craftsmen. Both chose to go to Ozark Technical College in Springfield. That's where they met and became good friends.

Steve was the smart one, the more polished one. He grew up in an upper-middle-class home on the south side of Springfield. His mother was a doctor. His father was a carpenter.

He used to tell people, "I got my intelligence and good looks from my mother. I got everything else from my dad."

He cruised through high school without really trying, was on the honor roll and could have gotten into almost any college he wanted. His passion for working with his hands pushed him to enroll at OTC.

His first love, his only love, was Becky Farmer. They met the summer before his sophomore year at Springfield Kickapoo High School. She was a cheerleader. He was a linebacker on the football team. But they didn't meet at school. They meet at a drive-in diner, a place both of them worked part-time summers, after school and weekends.

"There is something about Becky," he told his best friend, Karl. "She's attractive but not more so than a lot of other girls. But her smile and the look in her eyes is like no one else."

Steve told Karl the word he kept coming back to for her in his mind was "genuine."

"There is nothing fake about her," he said. "She's not pretending to be someone else."

Becky didn't feel the same way about Steve. Not at first. "He's a jock," she told a group of friends. "And even worse, he's a football jock. They all think they are God's gift. You can't trust them."

But Steve was persistent and goal-oriented. And his

persistence would eventually wear her down. He'd say "hi," and smile in the hallway. He'd say "hi," and smile by the water fountain, and he'd say "hi," and smile before the game against eastside rivals, Glendale.

"Is that all you do? Say hi and smile," she asked.

"Uh-huh," he said, smiling. And that's how it started. Mind you, school was not the first place they met. That was at Al's drive-in diner, where Becky worked as a carhop and Steve worked as a fry cook. Steve was smitten with her the first time he saw her.

Before their first date, he met Becky's parents. He was dressed in a blue suit, the one he wore to church every week. He brought flowers and chocolates for her mom. He wanted their permission before asking Becky to the dance. Steve didn't want her to have any easy outs.

"Mr. and Mrs. Jacobs, I'll have her home whenever you want, and I promise there will be no drinking or smoking," he said earnestly. "I will take good care of your daughter."

Impressed by his effort and calmed by his vulnerability, Becky's parents gave him the green light. Now, he had to convince Becky.

The fact was he was stalling. He was scared to ask her. Steve had never asked a girl out before, and his heart rate jumped just thinking about her saying no. Five days before the dance, he saw Becky talking to a few girlfriends after school. He waited quietly on a bench outside the front entrance about fifty feet away, fixing his shoelaces and winding his watch, hoping to catch Becky alone soon.

But one of Becky's friends spotted him winding his watch for a third time. She nudged others in the group, and one by one, they glanced his way, giggling.

He had to make his move now, no matter how embarrassing it was going to be. So, he slowly walked up to the group. They were all looking at him with grins on their faces in anticipation. All except Becky. She had a serious look on her face.

"Hi, girls," Steve said with his voice cracking. "Can I speak to Becky, please?"

Smiling, they backed away politely, careful to stay near enough to hear what he said.

Steve cleared his throat, smiled nervously and looked into Becky's eyes. He didn't know what she would say. *Had he embarrassed her as much as he had embarrassed himself,* he wondered. For a second, he wished he could be anywhere but standing in front of her right now with her friends just feet away.

Then he saw that something in her eyes again—that softness he had seen before, the thing that drew him to her. He knew without her saying so that she wanted him to talk. Without saying a word, she just looked him straight in the face, waiting. She knew what he wanted, and somehow knowing that calmed him down.

He took a deep breath and managed a small smile. "Becky, will you go to the dance with me?"

She smiled. "Yes, I will, Steve Raymond," with a touch of 'it's about time' in her voice. What her girlfriends heard just feet away didn't tell the story. It was all in the smiles.

And that was the real beginning of everything for them.

After high school, both remained in Springfield to be near each other. Becky attended college. Steve went to trade school. She wanted to be a teacher. He could see himself woodworking, so carpentry, he thought.

They continued to date and talk about their future together. But time away from each other began to pull them apart. They were consumed with themselves the way young adults often are. They had their goals and their new friends. One day they stopped talking about their future together. Slowly, one step at a time, other priorities took over. But much like their smiles when he asked her to the dance, they didn't talk about what had changed.

It was during this time, Steve's first year at OTC, he became friends with Gary Walker. Though they had lived just miles away from each other, the mobile home Gary grew up on the outskirts of Nixa was a world away from Steve's upbringing. Gary was an only child. His mother cleaned houses and worked at the local waffle house to make ends meet. His father was a drunk, a skirt-chaser who stayed away from home for days at a time. He worked at the 3M factory in Springfield until he got laid off the year Gary started high school.

Unemployment gave his father an excuse to drink more. He found a resting spot on a barstool at Duke's Tavern. He came home only when he was out of money. His dad would threaten and beat Gary's mother until she gave him enough money for him to leave. Gary got good at blocking out his dad and staying busy. If he couldn't leave, he'd just whittle on some wood with his pocketknife. He was good at ignoring confrontations. He learned how from his mom.

Sometime during Gary's sophomore year at Nixa High School, his father stopped coming home altogether. It was the start of a new chapter in his life. He was growing up fast now.

During his junior year, his mother suffered a stroke. She was unable to work after that. A small disability check and food stamps meant things were tight for the two of them. Gary dropped out of school to take care of her. He went to work washing dishes, cooking, cleaning, anything that paid him money.

"The worst part of it all," he told Steve one day, "was the look people gave me when I went into the local grocery store and paid for my food with food stamps. People can be so judgmental. They don't feel empathy for you. They only feel sorry for you."

When his friends graduated from high school, he began

studying to take his GED. He was determined to be his own man, to set his own course. It took him nearly a year to get his GED. Soon after, he enrolled at the tech school.

Gary was a year older than Steve but was light years ahead of him in life experiences.

Both were loners. Steve was shy and unsure of himself. He had many advantages but didn't see them. He was athletic, smart, and grounded, but he always had doubts. He was in a new school, a place where he knew no one. There were few girls, and most of the guys had split into various friend groups. Gary was talkative but awkward. A bully he knew in grade school called him Gomer Pyle. Gary was tall and lanky and had trouble getting words out, so it stuck for a while. Gary didn't like it but found it went away if he didn't fight it.

It was hard to keep Gary down. He always had a smile on his face and knew who he was, which is what drew Steve to sit across from him at lunch one day. They each had sat alone before.

"Hi, my name is Steve," he said, holding out his hand.

"Glad to know you, Steve. I'm Gary."

Despite their differences, the duo understood each other like no one else did. Steve felt it was an unspoken bond, like what he had with Becky. Both boys dreamed of becoming craftsmen, maybe working at Silver Dollar City after graduation or somewhere around Branson, where a quiet resort and vacation culture had taken root around the lakes. Things were beginning. Life was just getting started. They were both hopeful.

Steve and Gary took most of the same classes. They studied together and even worked at the same McDonald's after school and on weekends. After work, they would go to Billy Bobs, a local country and western bar that Gary liked to say was more country than western. Billy Bobs had seen better times. It was a dive bar, kept in business by workers at the local 3M plant that stopped in after their shift for a cold brew before going home.

Despite its lack of charm, the bar had a loyal following. Everyone seemed to know each other. They talked. They laughed. They forgot about their bills, their lives and their wives for a while. Steve and Gary felt it. They felt they belonged. It became their home away from home.

Gary lost his virginity to a barmaid at Billy Bobs. Her name was Rachael. She was forty-two, divorced three times and had four kids. The oldest was two years older than Gary. None of that mattered to Gary at the time, who was grateful for the female attention.

The bar owner said she had blonde hair too long for her age and a belly and boobs too large for her halter tops. Her make-up was always generously applied. Gary thought she was perfect.

They dated for nearly four months. Their dates mostly comprised brief rendezvous after closing time in the back of

Gary's pick-up truck at a secluded make-out spot in a park or by a creek. She felt young with Gary, and his attention was enough. She felt safe. She was in control. She couldn't remember a time when a man looked at her the way Gary did and meant it. And Gary meant it. He was in love almost immediately. She was entertained, and that was enough.

It was during the months they dated that Steve noticed a change in his friend. It was as if his personality was being swallowed up by hers. She ran the show, and he ran on her whistle. She had certain expectations. Rachael wanted Gary to provide. It was time a man took care of her, took care of her kids. It would be a stretch, though. He could barely take care of himself. He would scrape to get by, but he never had a good job. She knew it, but she was in denial. He could take care of her with her direction, she thought.

It was the Summer of '73, four months into their relationship when Rachael discovered she was pregnant.

Damn, why had I always been so fertile? she thought to herself. *Why didn't I make him use protection?*

She thought the last thing she needed right now was another mouth to feed. She was barely making ends meet as it was. And, the father would be of little help. Gary was about as poor as she was. And, with a baby in her stomach, her dreams of finding a man with the financial means to support her would need to be put on hold. *What man is going to chase me with a child in my stomach and four more at home?* she thought.

Rachael decided she'd have to fix the problem. She was too old for this. She couldn't have another kid. "And not with a kid!" Rachael decided to get an abortion and figured she would get Gary to pay for it.

Gary did not share her reaction to the news.

"The son of a bitch was fucking ecstatic," she told one of her friends.

Gary was ready to marry her. He wanted to raise her children. He wanted to step up and take care of her. That was when she knew she couldn't stay in denial. That's when she knew she'd have to break it off. First, however, wanted to take care of "the baby problem."

Rachael knew the key would be to convince Gary that the baby would get in the way of their love. Everything would change. He'd have to see it. She could make him see it.

It didn't go well initially. The idea of his girlfriend getting an abortion sickened him. "That's my baby. I can raise him. We can raise him together."

But the pressure mounted after she stopped seeing him, stopped answering his phone calls and began dating other men. He was feeling desperate. He needed her back. He'd do anything. So, reluctantly, he promised her he would get the money to pay for her abortion. He didn't know just how, but he'd figure out something. He had to.

Billy Bobs had two kinds of people that frequented the bar. It had the blue-collar workers, mainly from the 3M plant, who stopped in after their shift for a few cold beers and to shoot the shit with their friends before going home. But the dive bar was also a staple for drifters, hustlers, the kind willing to skirt the law to avoid a steady job. That group, predictably, had a lot of turnover. Those customers were constantly changing. Billy Bobs was a welcoming place where anyone tired of the grind could find refuge.

One particularly done-with-work type got Rachael's attention. His name was Harley, or at least that was what people called him. He rode a '63 Harley motorcycle with a muffler anyone could hear coming from blocks away.

Harley was hardened. He was over fifty with a long, gray beard and dirty blond hair pulled back into a ponytail. He had a sleeve of tattoos on both arms before that was a thing. He was thin and tall with muscular arms. He was fresh from prison, he bragged to Rachael, sensing her excitement.

She was to him what Gary was to Rachael. A thing to spin around and watch giggle. She hid her relationship from Gary at first. They'd meet late at night after Gary had gone home. Harley was a thrill for her. As much as she appreciated the control she had with Gary, Harley made her feel young in a different way. He was wild. He couldn't be controlled. And she loved it. She took everything she could get and loved it.

But she still needed Gary. Harley never pretended that he wanted anything more from Rachael than sex. He certainly wasn't going to pay for her abortion. So she needed Gary to believe they could still be together. She was being used and using.

One particular night, after Harley and Rachael broke into an abandoned north-side house and had sex, changed everything like a sudden Ozarks' storm.

"Have you ever heard of crank? Crystal? Meth?" Harley asked Rachael, lying with her on an open sleeping bag. These were the days before the cocaine-fueled disco craze. Harley had picked up tips on how to make "prison speed" during his lengthy incarceration. Now a free man, making meth from an assortment of toxic but cheap ingredients and selling it was his only ambition. This was Hillbilly cocaine —' a chemical brother to the amphetamines the Nazis took on blitzkrieg runs in World War II. Harley was speaking a deep-backwoods, racist's criminal language for 1973.

"It's some sort of drug, isn't it?" she replied, acting coy, assuming he was talking about uppers.

"Not just a drug," he said. "It's *the* drug. It's going to be the biggest drug there is. It gives the highest high. It's cheap. It's easy to make, and everyone is going to want it."

"What do you know about it?" she asked.

"I make it," he said quietly with a smile. "I got a place back in the deep woods, an isolated spot hidden from everything. I've got a crew that makes it. Hell, we sell it all as soon as we've got a batch. That shit is going to make me rich."

He liked looking into her eyes to see how she would

react. She smiled back at him. He knew she would. That's when he pulled out a small piece of crystal about the size of a pebble and handed it to her. It had a pinkish cloud to it, a substance that resembled a foggy glass or ice in moonshine. She looked it over, picked it up, smelled it, and moved it around her hand with the curiosity of an infant just learning how to walk.

"How do you get high from it?" she asked.

"There are several ways, but I'll show you the easiest way," he said, watching her closely. He put it on the floor next to them, and with a rock, he smashed it with the palm of his hand until it broke into a sandy, white powder. Then he pulled out his knife, put a few grains on the edge of the blade and lifted it to his nose. He snorted the substance into his nose and closed his eyes.

When he opened his eyes, he had a smile on his face, like a child that just experienced candy for the first time. What a show, he thought to himself, proud.

"Do you want to try it?" he asked Rachael.

"Yes," she replied without hesitation but a little terrified and thrilled.

Rachael had never gotten high beyond pot or a few uppers she took at a party once. She was a drinker. This was different. This was energy. It was instant coffee. It was a rush. This was the thrill she had riding on the back of his bike. Her mind was clear. She felt alive and aware, and sexy.

They made love again, but this time, her body was ultra-sensitive. Every movement, every touch of her lover, brought a new excitement. She was a kid again. She was being naughty with a bad boy. It was a feeling she thought she could never have again. She was content for a time. But the weather could change fast in the Ozarks.

CHAPTER 3
THE BAD BOY

Choices in his life had hardened Harley. His parents were drug addicts. Social services took him away when he was 5 years old. That began a succession of foster parents, each one seemingly worse than the other. He grew up on the south side of Chicago and joined a gang at the age of twelve. By the time he was fifteen, he had left home for good. The streets became his playground. Peddling drugs and small-time robbery became his career. Turf wars were common among gangs back then. Each gang wanted to control certain neighborhoods.

Each gang war was followed by a time of acceptance and agreement for a while. But that never lasted. Either one gang would get greedy and go after another's turf, or someone would cross the line and get hurt or hurt someone else. Each skirmish was followed by an appropriate response, a payback. Each payback resulted in an escalation, which would eventually result in war. It was a vicious cycle.

Harley was a warrior, a fighter. He got used to pain and could tolerate it more than others. He felt most comfortable and valuable when his gang was at war. He found he enjoyed watching others suffer and in making them suffer. He enjoyed inflicting pain. It gave him a rush. And he would find any little reason to do it. It made him a leader. It made him feared.

When a rival gang decided to expand their drug trade and extortion business into their territory, Harley was the person the gang tasked with doling out the payback. Knives and brass knuckles were the weapons of choice back then.

The attack happened late at night, under a full moon. A small group, four or five members of the other gang, had congregated outside a small family liquor store two blocks from his side's territory.

Harley led a group of twelve. The fight only lasted for a few minutes. When it was over, not a member of the rivals was left standing. Knife wounds and head wounds landed all but one in the hospital. The other gang member, a boy barely out of elementary school, was taken to the morgue.

At the age of eighteen, Harley had killed a thirteen-year-old member of a rival gang. The victim wasn't armed. He had no chance to fight back. His life was taken by a knife wound that penetrated an artery leading to his heart.

To avoid the consequences of his actions, Harley stole a car and headed south to a place no one was likely to find him. The Ozarks provided the isolation and obscurity to hide his secret for a long time.

Eventually, his drinking and inability to stop talking would be his downfall. He bragged about the killing on numerous occasions. Somebody turned him in. He never found out who it was. The law would catch up with him for the murder in Chicago. He was sentenced to thirty years altogether. He served eighteen before he was paroled. A couple of years later, a parole violation resulted in him returning to prison and completing his sentence. He had recently gotten out of prison when he bragged to Rachael. While he'd spent precious little time outside the federal fences in Marion, Ill. and Licking, MO., when it came to survival, hustling, and getting by on his wits, he was an Alpha, a dominant manipulator compared to Rachael.

Prison had molded him, hardened his shell. Familiar with "bennies" from his street days, he learned how to make the prison speed from a thief named Abe from Reeds Spring.

When Harley was released, he bought a '63 Harley Davidson motorcycle from the money he'd stolen and hidden before his parole violation and headed south of Springfield to connect with a couple of the people Abe talked about. He was determined to put his new skills to use.

On a secluded property high in the Ozark hills north

of Branson, he formed a business partnership with an acquaintance of his prison buddy, Abe. The acquaintance, a moonshiner named Tim, owned the property and had a working still that, with a few alterations, would be converted into a crude meth-making machine.

It took less than a week to convert the still. It took another week to produce the first batch of meth. Within a month, they could produce as much as two ounces a day.

Selling meth proved to be more challenging than making it. It was a new drug back then. Hill people were skeptical of outsiders. Tim became instrumental in getting the product in their hands. He had grown up in the Ozarks. Everyone knew him or had heard of him or knew someone that knew him. The first batches of meth they produced were given away at parties to good old boys from Tim's network of moonshine customers. Tim would vouge for Harley. And soon, out of fear or respect or both, Harley was thought of as a local not to be messed with. The high those customers got from meth was like nothing else they had ever experienced. Selling the product after that was relatively easy — though it was a select and rough market.

Harley figured he could sell ounces by the gram and easily make several hundred dollars per batch. But he'd have to use it with them first — show them how to crush it with his lucky Swan Creek flat stone — and get them craving more. Most people didn't know what meth was in those days.

Harley was ahead of his time, nurturing a budding addictive demand that would eventually take root.

Like many partnerships formed from greed and illicit behavior, theirs was doomed to fail. Abe was the weaker of the two partners. On a late, foggy night, after several hours of partying, Abe simply disappeared. He was never seen again. Rumors among the hill people were that Harley had murdered him, then buried him in a shallow grave in the middle of nowhere. Those, of course, were only rumors. Abe's body was never found.

When Harley needed to expand his base of customers, he'd frequent dive bars and find out where the seedy parties were. Ozarkers were sociable once they knew a name and face, and Harley found them eager to try a new high. All he needed was for folks to try it. *Then the rednecks will come to me when they want to party. Who else has what I got?*

As his little operation grew, it was easy to find free help getting his "Ozark Coke" out there. Harley found an abundance of addicted customers that would gladly work for meth to feed their addiction.

The foundation of Harley's drug ring wasn't built on a solid cornerstone, mind you. Mixing drugs and work resulted in mistakes both of mind and judgement. And the people lining up to work for Harley weren't angels. Some tried to steal from him, of course. Some were too high to get the product to where or whom it belonged.

Harley wasn't the forgiving boss, either. He had a way of making problems disappear in the dense backwoods that stretched across southern Missouri and northern Arkansas. There was no shortage of possible solutions for problems that cropped up in remote hills where distant gunshots were like friendly neighbors waving.

When it was time to play, Harley could pick from an ever-increasing supply of addicted female customers. He watched as their meth addiction transformed them from innocent, slightly naïve young girls with fresh, youthful faces and bodies into worn, hardened, desperate souls that aged way faster than their years.

His drugs satisfied the young women he supplied until their dependency forced them to satisfy him. Prostitution became an expansion of his business. The sprawling hotels, convention centers and nightspots of Branson and Springfield would become the quiet working ground of the most desperate of his addicted young female customers.

It was during one of his work-related trips to Springfield that he first entered Billy Bobs, where he first noticed Rachael. He had plans for her almost the minute he saw her. Harley had a way of spotting desperate people. Rachael wasn't addicted to drugs. He could see that. But she had an addiction, something that was pulling her to him, something he would be able to use against her.

He noticed her desires in the looks she gave him, her

smile, and her tender touch. The first time they made love was nothing short of animalistic lust. He took her against the wall at the rear of Billy Bobs just before sunrise, long after the last customer had left the bar.

Harley wasn't a particularly handsome man. He was on the downside of fifty, heavy set with graying hair. Rachael was over twenty years younger, in the prime of life, and attractive with the body of a twenty-year-old. But for some reason, she was drawn to him. Some toughness she recognized.

***

Rachel's addiction was pain, not physical, but emotional pain. She was drawn to men that were destined to leave, to hurt her. Harley was that kind of man.

Rachael had the sense to know that a real relationship with Harley was probably doomed to failure, but she couldn't resist their late-night meetings after Gary had left work. The fact that their rendezvous were secret gave the trists more power and appeal. There was a dark magnetism between them that was energizing to her. Still, she needed to keep responsible Gary around.

He was useful for a while. Rachael was a spider, and he was a meal wrapped in her web. And he'd give her what she needed.

While she could barely contain or control Harley, she had noticed his wads of cash. Oh, how she would love to get her hands on that money, to mean enough for him to give it to her, she thought. In many ways, she was repeating an arc of relationships past. The busty, friendly, bashful waitress just needs a little help with this month's rent or fixing a Buick or getting the lights put back on. Eventually, her type of bad boy would leave. It was happening again with Harley.

What if she could get more out of him? Money would solve most of her problems, she thought. She could begin a new life, a better life. She could move away from Springfield to Kansas City, or Tulsa or Wichita and start fresh like when she was younger. Maybe go to college. She could leave Billy Bobs behind.

Wasn't Harley scared of someone robbing him? she thought. *Maybe he should have been.*

But she needed to handle the problem growing in her stomach before she could even think of bigger dreams. And that wouldn't be easy. This was Greene County, the Bible belt of Missouri. No licensed doctor provided abortion services in that part of the state. She would need to travel to get it done or find someone in the Ozarks who would do it quietly. Rachael knew a server at Billy Bob's a couple of years earlier that used a guy out of Hollister to take care of her situation. Maybe she could give her his number.

To get the money, she would have to either put more pressure on Gary or find a way to get money from Harley.

The nights Harley came into the bar, she'd watch and listen intently to him, looking for an angle. That's when it dawned on her: Billy Bobs was the key. She'd have Gary rob Harley.

She couldn't trust Gary to help craft her plan, of course. *I'll have to map out everything for him*, she thought. And she knew she couldn't afford for Harley to know she was involved. He would kill her. She knew it.

So, she took her time. She thought it out between slinging pints and drafts. And she'd discreetly ask as much of Harley as she could after sex when he was most talkative. She'd make note of everything he told her. Soon, she discovered that he had several middlemen. He referred to them as "mules." He was usually visiting them on the same nights he was visiting her. That's when he had to be dropping off drugs and picking up money.

Damn, she thought to herself, *he's got the money I need on the nights he's here.*

And Harley had already given her a taste for meth. She realized her bad boy had more than just money to offer. Maybe Gary could take more than money. Maybe this fly was juicier than she thought.

CHAPTER 4
SCHOOL DAYS

Sitting on that bench overlooking Lake Honor, I pondered what had brought me back to this place. For over forty years, I had purposely stayed away. The memories were too painful. I wanted to forget them. I had nearly let those memories die.

It was old friends who had come back into my life. I'd received a Facebook message from two friends out of nowhere and within two weeks of each other. I hadn't heard from either in four decades.

One was a girl I had met during my freshman year at S of O. I had fallen hard for her in the fall of '73. She was curious about how life had treated me. I was excited to hear from her. She had been married for forty years, was retired, had two grown children and was a grandmother. As she talked about her life, the bubble I had put my memories of her in began to deflate. I suddenly realized that time had not frozen in the year 1973. I had pictured Erin exactly how I last saw her: a bubbly, vibrant nineteen-year-old with long, flowing brown hair and crisp blue eyes.

She had grown old just as I had. She was doing well, and I was thankful for that. We were both happy and content with how our lives had evolved.

Predictably, the conversation turned to our days at S of O. She had continued there and graduated, then gone on to become a teacher. Her memories of the school were much better than mine. She had gone back many times for homecoming, basketball games, and different events.

She talked about friends. Most, I couldn't remember. "Amazingly, the school looks just like it did back then. Nothing has really changed," she said.

Eventually, the conversation drifted to that day in October when the two bodies were discovered floating in Lake Honor.

"Do you remember that day?" she asked.

"Yes, I remember."

Two dead boys floating in the heart of a tight-knit campus wasn't the kind of thing people forgot.

"Didn't you write a story about the death of those two boys?" she asked.

"Yes, that was a long time ago," I said in a direct tone.

I didn't want to talk about it.

We wrapped up the conversation soon after, and that was the last time we talked. It's as if that day represented some dirty secret we shared, and to talk about it was violating some code of discretion to make light of the memory. At least, it was for me. And if it was no big deal to her, I didn't want to know. Yet the fact that she brought the memory up told me that I was not the only one who could not forget or let the memories of that day die.

Two weeks later, my best friend from S of O, my roommate and my best man at my wedding contacted me on Facebook. I hadn't seen or talked to him for thirty-five years. Our relationship died just about the time that my first marriage collapsed. My first wife was a student at S of O. We met there in December of '73, just before I left the school for good. She was a kind person, gentle, easy-going, honest, happy and innocent—just like most of the Ozarks people I met.

It seemed the ghosts of my past were gathering around me.

Charlie Ross was my best friend. He also grew up in the Ozarks. There was nobody more loyal, more genuine than Charlie. I don't know why we lost touch with each other. It's been too many years to remember the reason. I suspect it was me. I had changed. I wasn't an easy person to like anymore.

He was friends with my ex-wife through Facebook. I

never realized that until we started talking again. He was the same guy I remembered: happy, never complaining, funny and always optimistic.

His life had not gone as well as I had hoped. Life had been tough for him, but I don't think he would ever admit it. His health had deteriorated. He rarely left the house now. He was divorced, alone. He had two grown daughters, but I sensed they had moved away and rarely contacted him anymore. He hadn't changed, but things weren't easy for him.

As I mentioned, we connected through Facebook. Over time, by reading his posts and comments from his friends, I realized that he had lived a full life and was quite popular. That didn't surprise me. Charlie had a heart of gold. He was the type of person who always made you feel good. He was the type of person everyone wanted to be around. And I was encouraged to know it.

As a freshman away from home for the first time, I didn't immediately connect with Charlie. He was a likable guy, but we didn't seem to have anything in common. He had grown up in a small town in the hills of the Ozarks. He enjoyed hunting, fishing, drinking, and partying in general. I was a jock who grew up in the city. Before I met him, I hadn't even had a beer before. I was the city boy, but I was the conservative one. I only cared about two things then: running and studying. I missed my mother's cooking. I missed the smell of his father's pipe in the family room. I missed the laughter of my home in Kansas City. I was even beginning to miss my little brother, Dennis. He was six years younger than me and constantly getting into my stuff.

I had looked forward to going away to college for so long. I thought that I was ready for my freedom, my independence. I never realized how much I would miss those times when I was so anxious to leave. Most of all, I missed Nancy.

I dated Nancy during my senior year. She was a junior. We met while working together at Taco Bell. We both worked evenings and weekends to put gas in our cars and save money for college. We became friends first and then began dating. She was smart, funny and attractive. She was my first real love. Looking back, she represented home for me. And now I was in this foreign place. The Ozarks were completely alien to me. It was a place where people were kind yet secretive; humble, determined; wise, and liked to play dumb. The people of the Ozarks would spell words on billboards backward and talk in Hillbilly wearing overalls for city folk like me who visit and call it country charm, all while raking in their money at Pressley's or Silver Dollar City. It was a place of contradictions, and I wasn't sure if I belonged.

I had left my family, friends and girlfriend for a place that seemed so isolated, that felt so lonely. I remember the days were tolerable. Classes, studying and training kept me plenty busy. And being busy was good. I was surrounded by people. But nights were agonizing. I was in a tiny, cold, dark dormitory room with a roommate I didn't know, nor did I particularly like at first. I didn't understand Charlie.

School seemed like a vacation to him. He partied late almost every night. He skirted the rules. Charlie had so many friends, and our room was the gathering point for them. Their routine was nearly the same every night. After school, they would congregate in our room to make plans for the evening. There were always parties going on around the lakes during the early days of Fall.

They would decide which ones to go to. Or maybe, they just grab a six-pack or two and go down to the lake. No one in his group of friends was of legal age to drink, but Charlie had a believable fake ID. And that, combined with his looks, a man several years older than nineteen normally was enough to get him what he wanted at the area liquor stores.

Track and cross-country practice would normally last until 6 p.m. or so. Then I'd eat in the cafeteria, and afterward, I'd go to the library to study. By 8 p.m., the group in my room was usually cleared out, and I'd return to the dorm. There were times that I would get upset with Charlie, mainly when he'd come back to the room late and wake me from a sound sleep. But I could never stay mad very long. There was something about his personality that made it impossible to stay mad with him. I never saw him angry. I never heard him say a bad word about anyone. He was happy-go-lucky all the time.

I had very little in common with most of the students. Looking back on it now, I was a bit of a snob. It wasn't that I thought that I was better than anyone else. I just felt that I was different. I was a city boy, living his entire life in the suburbs of Kansas City.

Most of the other students grew up in rural Missouri or Arkansas and enjoyed the simple pleasures of life: fishing, hunting, and drinking. I grew up in a middle-class family. I had only fished once in my life and had never gone hunting. I enjoyed what the city had to offer, malls, fast food restaurants, baseball and football and plenty of movie theatres. The Ozarks offered none of those things. I felt I was their fish out of water.

S of O was deep in the Ozarks, just 10 miles from the Arkansas border. All the students who attended the school worked for it. Students worked a minimum of twenty hours per week to pay for their tuition, room and board. Most students worked additional hours to pay for incidentals.

The student body consisted predominantly of young men and women who had struggled in life. Most were first-generation college students. Their parents couldn't afford a traditional education for their children. S of O was a blessing. Only about one in eight students who applied for admission was accepted. Church, work and education, very much in that order, were the focal points of campus life.

Freedoms were limited. Students could not have cars

on campus. There was a student lot off-campus. It was locked from 9:30 p.m. to 8 a.m. every night. Dormitories were locked up at 10 p.m. on weekdays and 11p.m. on weekends. Students had to be in their rooms when the dormitory was locked down. There were dress codes that required women to wear dresses and men to wear slacks or khakis with button-down shirts.

Attendance at all classes and school-sponsored events was mandatory unless there was an excused absence. Rules were strict and inflexible. Expulsions were a common punishment. S of O was a no-nonsense college. It was a privilege to be accepted, and to get a quality, free education. Graduates had little trouble getting jobs, although most job offers tended to come from businesses in or near the Ozarks. In recent years, the College of the Ozarks had become known as a cultural and political hub for Christian conservatism. Nicknamed Hard Work U., the Keeter Center at Point Lookout had hosted speakers including Fox News' Bill O'Reilly, President George W. Bush, Prime Minister Margaret Thatcher and General Colin Powell, among others. It was, in many ways, always aiming to be a shining light on a hill.

In my time, most students conformed to the rules and standards the school required. They realized what a wonderful opportunity the school had given them. Some, a small minority of the student body, resisted conformity. Usually, they were weeded out in a quick fashion.

Every student, during their first day of orientation, was assigned a job on campus. Many worked in jobs for which they had experience or had demonstrated an aptitude. But faith came first. The student body was hand-picked for their Christian values, and job skills were secondary. Students just needed to be prepared to learn and work.

S of O was unique from any other college in that the campus was completely self-sufficient. It didn't rely on outside services. Everything needed to operate the school was done on campus. Further, the school sold products they developed to outside stores and businesses. And it generated considerable revenue from those sales. This was its dirty secret. This was how the school made its money. A free education meant you hustled. And like so much else in these hills and valleys, the secret was no secret. No one hid from the truth. The truth lay bare in the open.

Being where it was, even in the 70s, it was a tourist attraction. Nestled just south of Branson and the Silver Dollar City resort areas, S of O had a very popular restaurant on campus, a large general store that sold items students made, as well as a bakery and ice cream shop the students ran. It had a Christian bookstore and a small bed and breakfast that was booked months in advance. The tourist area was contained on the northern edge of campus, away from the dormitories and classrooms. But separated or not, it was always more than a center for learning or a fountain of faith. It was big business, too.

On Sundays, visitors flocked to campus for a church service dedicated just to them. Students attended church at 7 a.m. on Sundays. At 11 a.m., a special service took place at the stone chapel. That service was for visitors and alumni only. Colorful flowers were brought in to ordain every corner of the church. The student choir, in full gowns, were present. The service took on a spirit reminiscent of a fine tele-evangelist service. The entire service was a production designed to impress the visitors into giving large donations and departing with some of their disposable income. It worked very effectively. The campus restaurant and stores were packed for the remainder of Sunday afternoons.

The school's administrators were geniuses at marketing. Sure, they gave their students and the parents exactly what they promised, a quality, Christian-based education centered around a strong work ethic. But, first and foremost, they sold a utopian view of life on campus. The school's reputation was impeccable, and they did whatever was necessary to keep it that way.

From an outsider's point of view, S of O appeared remarkable. They had their own police and fire departments, an electrical plant on campus provided all the needed electricity and even sold the excess back to local communities. They had a sprawling farm that raised cattle, hogs, chickens and turkeys that were slaughtered to provide food for the students while excess meat was sold to local restaurants and grocery stores. They raised vegetables and fruit trees and had the largest dairy farm in the area. The campus had its own canning facility and a large pond where catfish were harvested and appeared on the menu at the campus restaurant. It was farm-to-table long before that was a trend. There was a tailor shop that made clothes that were sold in their gift shop. Every job on campus was done by students. It was like no other college in America. The school accumulated great wealth over the years, but it was a quiet wealth. It was a wealth few people knew about. The image they portrayed was that of a struggling college in desperate need of donations and support. While it was a beautiful place, the campus always had things in need of repair. That was exactly the image they wanted outsiders to have of S of O.

Donations came into the school from all over the country. It was a college that people wanted to believe in. It provided free education to students that desperately needed it. But, more than that, S of O provided education to the right students, the cream of the crop, the students that were most deserving, the students that would make good citizens and good Christians.

S of O was a success story like no other. They had worked hard to groom their reputation, and they worked equally hard to maintain it. There was always a darkness behind the façade that the administration tried so hard to maintain. It was a darkness that crept through the underbelly of campus life. It was a darkness that few knew anything about. It was a darkness that I would soon discover.

I came to S of O because I had nowhere else to go. My parents couldn't afford to send me to college.

A few months earlier, I hoped I'd get an athletic scholarship that would pay for all or most of my college education. Several college coaches were talking to me. I had a successful cross-country season in the fall and had done well during the indoor track season earlier in the year. Everything looked bright. I had talked to several college coaches. I felt that an athletic scholarship was in my grasp. Then, I got sick. Doctors found inflammation around my heart. And my unexpected setback would take months to fully heal. My scholarship hopes disappeared. After my older brother Ron told me about S of O, I talked to their cross-country coach, Trey Marks, who had led the team to the NAIA Nationals or sent at least one runner for six consecutive years.

The school did not give out athletic scholarships, although they did reduce work requirements for student athletes. There was one big catch, though: I would need to go through the same process as all the other applicants for acceptance. I had to get a recommendation letter from my minister. I had to provide recommendations from my principal, employer, and five others. My parents would need to show tax returns and provide financial information to show that they could not afford to pay for college tuition.

I completed everything that was required, and then I waited. Two weeks went by. Finally, Coach Marks phoned me.

"You've been accepted, Alan," he said. "You need to be here August 3 to get set up and begin training."

The day I was scheduled to leave for school, my girlfriend Nancy showed up to say goodbye. I hoped she would, but I didn't expect it. After all, we had agreed to part ways when I left for college. I packed my '69 cherry red Volkswagen Beetle, said goodbye to my parents, gave Nancy a final, tearful kiss and drove the nearly two hundred and fifty miles south to S of O. Hard work was waiting.

I received my work assignment the second day I was on campus. I was assigned to the Ozark Family Restaurant. It was the visitor and guest restaurant at the entrance to campus. I had a unique talent that was in need at the restaurant: I could drive a stick shift. The Volkswagen I drove was a three-speed. That talent came in handy at the restaurant. Supplies and deliveries for both the restaurant and the adjacent gift shop were made in a ten-year-old, beat-up Ford van that had a standard transmission and a challenging stick shift.

I soon discovered the delivery van was every bit as temperamental as my beetle had been when I first learned to drive it. But, in a short time, I was able to get around well without stalling out or jumping with every shift.

Making deliveries and picking up supplies was an easy job. Others loaded the van, and others emptied it. All I had to do was drive ten hours a week, most of that on weekends. My deliveries enabled me to see how vast the campus was. Most people had no idea how vast the school property was. S of O had quietly accumulated hundreds of acres of surrounding land over the years, stretching to the mountains on two sides and including most of the valley area nestled between three lakes.

The dairy was in the far northeast corner of campus, down a winding dirt road where there were fields of corn, wheat, barley and soy on either side. About a mile onto the dirt road was a large wire fence with a gate. It was locked. I had been given a key to unlock it. The wire fence ran the entire perimeter of the campus. Until my first delivery to the dairy farm, I had assumed the wire fence marked the end of S of O's property line. I was wrong. The school's property went well beyond the wire fences. The dairy farm was huge, extending another two miles or so beyond the fence line.

One oddity I noticed about the farm — its workers were older, local laborers. They weren't students. I had been told all work positions on the campus were filled by students. To the north of the dairy farm were the transportation building and lot. S of O had its own fleet of school buses and vans that were used for school travel, mainly by the athletic department for transporting athletes to various events.

Cross Country training began the second day I was on campus. Coach Marks had arranged for my work assignments to be flexible so as not to interfere with practice or classes. S of O was accommodating in that regard. Every job on campus worked around classes, athletic schedules and church.

A strong Christian education was the promise of S of O to all prospective students and their parents, and the Stone Chapel was the centerpiece of that effort. The church was founded in 1905 by Rev. James Forsythe, a Presbyterian missionary focused on filling the need he saw in the area for a Christian education. From the beginning then, hard work and disciplined living were expected.

For me, no one person embodied the local work ethic like Coach Marks. His workouts were legendary and brutal.

The intensity of Coach Marks's workouts far exceeded anything I experienced in high school. We worked out two and three times a day, running up hills, on backroads, climbing stairs, on the track, and in the gym. They left me exhausted and in terrible pain. My leg muscles tightened up at night, making it difficult to walk. After dinner, I went to the library, studied for a while, then returned to the dorm and went straight to bed. But the workouts were paying off. I was in the best shape I had ever been in. My heart was strong, and my legs were running harder and faster than any time before. And yet, it felt like I was on an island. Or a work camp for felons. My life had become work, run, sleep, repeat. Being on the team was a lonely existence.

There were plenty of attractive girls at S of O. They were different from the girls I had been used to in high school in that they didn't seem to be pretentious. By that, I mean the girls around campus seemed to have a wholesomeness about them that I found refreshing. If a man was looking for a wife, a life partner, he could do a lot worse than the girls on the campus of S of O.

Mind you, I certainly wasn't looking for a relationship. By the end of practice each day, I could barely get up enough energy to eat dinner, study and crawl into bed. Girls were the least of my interests, I thought.

That was until I met Erin. We had a chance meeting. I was on a work assignment picking up ice cream and bakery goods early one Saturday morning for the restaurant. The bakery was my first stop. I didn't want the ice cream to sit too long in the van. It was an unusually warm day for late September, and I didn't want to chance it starting to melt before I got back to the restaurant.

I backed into a small dock at the rear of the bakery. I knew I would only be a few minutes, so I left the engine running. That cranky old van could be challenging to start sometimes, so I didn't want to chance it.

Ordinarily, I would never need to go into the bakery. Normally the order for the restaurant would be waiting for me just inside the back door, but not that day. It wasn't there.

So, I walked into the bakery. That's when I saw her behind the counter. She was beautiful, with long flowing brown hair, crisp blue eyes and a smile that would have melted an ice cube.

That began a relationship that left me with fond memories throughout my life. There was a chemistry between us that I had never felt before. I had always been a bit of a hopeless romantic, believing that everyone had a sole mate, a person they were destined to spend the rest of their lives with.

Our feelings and our love were intense. We spent many nights together, on the shores of Lake Honor, under the tall oak trees, watching the fountain. It was so peaceful there. Life's problems and stresses seemed to resolve themselves on its shores. Young lovers met and planned their futures together there. We had no idea of the storm coming over the horizon.

That's where I found myself on that stormy night six weeks into my stay at S of O. A nearby lightning strike knocked the power off on campus. The lights were out in Rowlison Hall, and most of the students, flashlights in hand, gathered in the corridor outside their rooms. Charlie was there, too.

"I thought you'd be out partying," I said when I saw him.

"Na, not tonight, buddy. It's a mess out there," he replied.

After thirty minutes or so, the storm began to let up. The wind was no longer howling. The thunder was softer now, more distant. Finally, the lights began to flicker, and then they came back on. Students headed back to their rooms. So, did me and Charlie.

But there was something different about our room this time. The light from the fountain across the way from his window was not on.

"The fountain must not have gotten its power back yet," Charlie said.

I lay in bed, trying to relax, trying to forget about the pain in my quadriceps and shins that was pounding, trying to go to sleep. "Maybe it's clogged or something."

"Maybe," Charlie said.

"Whatever it is, it's not our problem," I said. I closed my eyes and drifted off into a deep sleep.

CHAPTER 5
A DARK PLACE

My father died two weeks after the bodies were discovered floating in Lake Honor. My mother called asking me to come home. I could tell by her voice that something was wrong, but she wouldn't say what it was. I'm sure she didn't want me driving home upset. But, from the cracking of her voice, I knew whatever happened was not good.

I left campus the next morning and headed home. When I arrived, the house was full of relatives. Everything went silent when I walked in the front door. I remember seeing my brother Ron and his wife. Ron lived only a few miles from S of O's campus, and he rarely ever came to Kansas City.

Then I saw the tears in my mother's eyes. I heard the soft cries. My mother took me by the hand and led me into the bedroom. "I have some terrible news," she said, wiping away a tear. "Your father has died."

Much of what happened for the next several days were foggy. We went to the funeral home. I saw his body in the casket. We went to the cemetery and watched him put into the ground.

I was never very close to my father. He was a good man, but he was quiet and distant. He worked hard, and he provided for his family.

I could not remember him ever being sick. But then again, he wouldn't have told anyone if he was. He was a strong man, a prideful man. He didn't complain about anything. I can only remember him crying once. That was the day President Kennedy was assassinated.

He lived life simply. A massive heart attack took his life at the age of forty-one.

His death and, in a way, the deaths of those two boys in Lake Honor changed my life. I was not the same person when I returned to school two weeks later.

I began to live life as if there might not be a tomorrow. I had no interest in being told what to do. Running was no longer very important to me, and neither was going to church. I blamed God for taking my father at such a young age. I began to rebel against any authority.

I drank for the first time. I smoked pot. I broke curfew and partied whenever I could. A dark side of me emerged.

I stopped caring about anyone but myself and whatever immediate self-gratification I could find.

Charlie and I became best friends. In fairness, he helped me get through that difficult time. He was a good friend. He listened to me. He supported me. He didn't judge me.

My running suffered. I was rebellious. I refused to listen to the coach or anyone on the team. The friendships that I had built with team members early in the semester evaporated.

I had started dating Erin in early September. She was beautiful with a great heart, empathetic, and caring. She was different from any of the girls I had met at S of O. She had drive, energy and a contagious smile. She was the type of girl that I could have married someday. I pushed her away after I came back to campus. Or maybe she pushed me away. It doesn't matter. She deserved someone better than I was back then.

Sex and drinking became my priorities. I made a lot of bad choices. There were many good people on that campus that I hurt or disappointed. I became self-centered. I used people.

The darkness in the waters of Lake Honor pulled on me. I no longer saw hope and innocence in the ripples the fountain pushed gently towards the shore. I was lost. At the center of my fountain was pain, and life offered no rest from it besides temporary pleasures. So that's what I sought.

I would drink. I would chase women. Women that

grew up in the Ozarks were different from the ones I'd known before. They were honest and faithful, with strong church and family values. It didn't take a lot to make them happy. It took even less to break their hearts. I wasn't trying to hurt others. I wasn't thinking about them. I just wanted to mask what I was feeling.

Erin was my biggest regret. I used her. I took her innocence on the shore of Lake Honor, underneath a large oak tree. It was what we both wanted at the time. She was falling in love. I was seeking anything that would soften the pain inside me.

Our relationship ended shortly after. She was smart. She saw me struggling with my demons before I knew they were there. It was tough. I felt I had nowhere to turn. Before the deaths, my new life in this new and very different place was hard. After, it felt impossible. I was barely holding on.

Given a little time and reflection, Lake Honor and I reconnected. That's where I could turn. We became kindred spirits. We had both been contaminated. We were both at the mercy of God and man and these unforgiving hills. This was my teammate. And as the vibrant colors of dying leaves fell from the tall oak trees baring winter-ready branches, I too felt its calm waters turn restless. The cool breeze that came off the lake and blanketed the shores in the still-warm summer and early fall months was gone, replaced by cold winds and nowhere to hide.

And the winter weather of '73 was harsh. A chilling fog engulfed the campus for days at a time. The winds howled, and the snow fell. I can still remember the cold. It was like nothing I had felt before. But it was the heavy grayness that hung all around and the quiet, the ever-present quiet of winter in the remote hills, that bothered me more.

It was death all around me. The death of my innocence, my childhood, my father, my peaceful lake, my budding relationship, my goals, my hope, the air and trees and ground.

When I left at the end of that fall semester, I didn't tell anyone. I didn't realize then that a piece of my soul would always remain on the shores of Lake Honor. I just had to leave. I couldn't stay under those clouds.

There was a wonderful girl named Katy that I met shortly before leaving. This was my first wife. She was kind, gentle, smart and sweet. She'd eventually follow me back to the Kansas City area. We married a year later. We had two children, both boys. Eventually, our marriage would fall apart. I've often said the failure of our marriage was nobody's fault. We just drifted apart. But that wasn't true. It was mainly my fault. I got married too young. I hadn't experienced enough of life on my own, and there was a restlessness inside me I couldn't deny, and she couldn't calm. The death of my father and those two boys who turned up in that lake were never far away—constant reminders of my own mortality. Mourning was replaced by a sense of urgency to live. I had no patience for patience. Whatever I had to do, I had to do it now.

It was Katy that encouraged me to write about the deaths of those two boys. I think now that she thought somehow that writing about my experience would close that chapter and release that anxiety inside of me.

I began to research the drowning of the two boys. Surprisingly, there was very little written about it. I found a couple of paragraphs in the Branson weekly paper and an obituary notice in that Springfield News-Leader that eluded to a suspicious death.

I knew little more than their names were Steve Raymond and Gary Walker. Their cause of death was determined to be drowning. There was no investigation. Their deaths were ruled accidental.

Several drownings happen yearly in the Lakes surrounding S of O. They get very little attention and certainly didn't warrant an investigation.

Forget that both the boys were fully clothed when they emerged from the bottom of Lake Honor. Forget that neither boy attended S of O or, to anyone's knowledge, had any connection with the college. Forget that the boys lived nearly fifty miles away, and no one knew how they got to campus. No car was left behind. Forget that the campus of S of O was gated, with no easy way to get inside without a student identification or visitor's pass.

If a person was inclined to swim, fully clothed, in a

lake late at night, there were three lakes in the area, not on private property, not patrolled by campus police, and not surrounded by gates and fences that would have been much easier to get to.

I had a lot of questions and no answers. I needed to understand what had happened. There was a real story here, and I needed to know what it was. My anxiety, and my frustration, suddenly had a purpose.

I contacted Steve Raymond's parents. We talked on the phone. They were receptive to talking to me. More than that, I think they were anxious to speak to someone about what happened to their son and his best friend.

I reached out to Gary Walker's mother only to discover that she had passed away. It seemed poor health and a broken heart claimed her life at a young age.

So, at 19, I packed a bag, loaded up my tape recorder and notebook, and took my first trip back to the Ozarks. I was nervous on the drive down to Springfield. I wasn't sure what to expect. I wasn't sure how receptive the Raymond family would be to my questions. I wasn't sure what their expectations of me would be. I wasn't a real reporter. No one was paying me for this story. It wasn't going to appear in the Kansas City Star, the Springfield News-Leader or any major publications for that matter, or at least I knew that couldn't be expected. And I could not give them hope of discovering the truth. I was simply trying to find closure in my life. I wanted to stop being haunted by the memories.

I half believed they would throw me out of the house when they sat down with me. I was no one. How could they trust I could provide them the answers they desperately needed? And if they couldn't, why bother talking to me? And what could I find out that they didn't already know?

I followed the directions they had given me to their home. It was a nice, middle-class neighborhood, row after row of brick-front ranch homes with one-car garages. The yards were well-manicured, and every lot was about the same size. The houses looked very similar. It was a planned neighborhood, much like many neighborhoods built immediately after World War II. Back then, a one-car garage was a luxury. Most houses had carports.

The nearby area had been swallowed up with progress: a large indoor mall three blocks away, a new school down the street, thoroughfares with gas stations, fast food restaurants and strip malls.

In a way, that neighborhood reminded me of S of O. It had not changed over time even though progress had surrounded it.

I pulled up in front of the house, took a deep breath, grabbed my recorder and notebook and walked up to the front door. I knocked softly on the door at first, not wanting to disturb the solemnness I expected to find inside.

No one answered, so I knocked a little louder. "I'm

coming," I heard a woman's voice say. The door opened, and a small, frail-looking older lady with short gray hair smiled at me from the other side of the screen door. "Come in," she said. "You must be Alan."

"Yes, I am. Is good to meet you, Mrs. Raymond."

"Please call me Dorothy," she said with a smile. "Come in. My husband Earl is in the living room. Earl, come out here. That nice boy from St. Joseph is here."

A few seconds later, Earl stepped into the hallway. He was a large man, tall and stout. His hair was almost completely gone, and what remained was gray and scattered. His face was worn and wrinkled. His eyes were sad. He tried to smile, but all he could manage was softening his facial muscles.

"Hello, young man," he said, holding out his hand to shake.

I couldn't help but notice that he dragged one leg when he walked, and his speech was a little slurred. Every step he took was calculated, slow.

"Earl had a stroke a few months ago," his wife said when he wasn't around. "The loss of our son has been hard on both of us."

Dorothy Raymond was talkative. She enjoyed talking about her son, particularly the good times she remembered. She talked about his first love, his only love, Becky Jacobs. "I was certain they would marry someday. Becky was his childhood sweetheart. They loved each other. After Steve's death, she came over almost every day. We'd sit and talk, mainly about Steve. She made dinner once in a while and ran errands for us if we needed something. Neither Earl nor I felt much like going out in public. People meant the best. But we just got tired of talking to people about what happened to our son. After a couple of months, I guess Becky got tired of thinking about the past too. She stopped coming around. We can't blame her. We found out she transferred to a college back East. She was a good person. I have no doubt that she loved our son. We were too busy dealing with our own pain to realize the pain she must have been going through too."

"Dorothy, what do you think happened to your son?" I asked.

"I think he and the other boy were murdered," she said, wiping a tear from her cheek.

I was taken aback by that answer. It wasn't a surprise she felt that way necessarily, but "murder" was a strong word. She didn't soften the word. She didn't change her tone. She didn't change the expression on her face. It wasn't the first time Dorothy had said it. I could tell it was a word she had used to describe her son's death before.

Her husband, Earl, showed no emotion. He just rocked back and forth in his chair, staring into space. I didn't know if it was his stroke that had made him so stoic or if he had grown tired of re-living the past.

"Mr. McLain says that our boy was involved in drugs,

and that was what led to his death. But I don't believe it. Steve was a good boy. He didn't drink, and he sure as hell didn't take drugs."

"Who is Mr. McLain?" I asked.

"He's the private detective we hired to find out what happened to our son. I think he is still working on it. I don't know for sure. It's been several weeks since we talked to him. All I know is that he is wrong when he says our son was involved with drugs. I can believe that of the other boy, Gary. He was bad news, a troublemaker. I don't know what Steve saw in him, how they could become friends. That, I don't think I will ever understand. Our son was guilty of bad judgement. That I can accept. But he wasn't into drugs. I will always believe that Steve was murdered because of something Gary did."

She suddenly stopped talking, but she was looking directly into my eyes as if she was trying to gauge how I would react to something she was going to say.

"Would you excuse me for a minute?" she finally said.

"Yes, of course," I replied.

She was gone for about five minutes. When she returned, she sat down next to me on the couch. I could tell she had been crying. She took her right hand and put it on my leg gently. She was grasping something in her left hand. I couldn't tell what it was.

"I told you about Becky before. She was my son's

first love, his only love as far as I knew. But I didn't tell you everything. After Steve's death, Becky and I got very close. She shared things about my son that I had never known before. They were deeply in love. They talked about marriage after Becky graduated from college and Steve started his career. Sometime toward the end of summer, after graduation, Becky became pregnant. She had only been with one man. That was my son, so there was no doubt who the father was. She never told my son. She said they weren't ready to get married and was certain that if she told Steve, he would insist on marrying her. I'm sure he would have too. Steve was that kind of person. So Becky found someone that would give her an abortion, and she took care of it.

"I could tell by her shaking voice and the tears that it was a heart-wrenching decision for her. She was haunted by those memories. Becky handed me a picture that day. It was a sonogram picture of the baby. She told me that she wanted me to have it."

She opened her left hand and handed the picture to me.

"I have no use for it anymore. The memories are just too painful. Please take it. Maybe it will provide you some comfort in trying to find the truth of what happened to my son."

I tried to turn her down. That picture was personal to her, to Steve's family. But she was insistent, and I accepted it.

Before leaving that day, I got the name and phone number of the private detective. He had been investigating the deaths for nearly a year. I figured I needed to talk to the private detective if I was going to get to the truth of what happened to Steve Raymond and Gary Walker. His name was Booger McLain.

I checked into a motel room in Springfield late that afternoon. I called him as soon as I got settled, not expecting him to answer the phone. I thought a secretary, an answering service, or perhaps an answering machine would pick up. But I was wrong. My preconceptions of what a private detective would look and act like soon would go out the window.

"Hello, you've reached Booger. How can I help you?" a loud, gruff voice answered.

"My name is Alan," I answered in a voice that reflected my age and nervousness. "I'm doing a story about the deaths of Steve Raymond and Gary Walker."

"I can't be of any help to you, son," he said in a voice that echoed, in a short tone that suggested he didn't give a shit.

"I don't think you understand, Mr. McLain," I said. "I was given your name by the Raymond family. They said you could help me understand what happened to those two boys."

"So, you've talked to the Raymonds, huh?" he asked, although it sounded more like a statement. "I'm surprised

Dorothy even brought my name up. She wasn't exactly thrilled with the way my investigation was going.

"Say, how's Earl. Is he doing any better?"

"I really don't know. He didn't really say anything."

"Yeah, that stroke really messed him up. I feel sorry for the Raymonds, but I don't think they'll ever accept that their son got mixed up with the wrong people."

"That's what I want to talk to you about, Mr. McClain. I want to get to the truth of what happened."

"Shit, son. No one wants to hear the truth. The police, the school where those boys drown, and even the parents. They all want to live in a world where things like that don't occur, where good people remain, good people, all their lives, and there is always a rainbow at the end of a rainstorm."

"Look, Mr. McLain. I want to get to the truth. I was there last year, at the school, when those bodies floated to the top of Lake Honor. I saw them fully dressed. I know that what happened to those boys was not an accidental drowning. I just want to hear what you have to say, Mr. McLain."

"Call me Booger," he said. There was a pause. I didn't have a clue about what he was going to say. "Where are you staying?" he asked after a few seconds.

"The Bel Air Motel on 67," I said.

"Geez, kid. Couldn't your newspaper afford anything better than that?" he asked.

"I don't work for a newspaper," I said. "I'm sort of

freelancing, I guess you'd say."

"Got enough money for a cup of coffee?" he asked.

"Yes."

"Good, I'll pick you up at 7a.m. What's your room number?"

"Two," I replied.

"See ya in the morning, kid."

CHAPTER 6
BOOGER MCLAIN

I couldn't have written a believable script with Booger McLain in it, but he belonged in a novel. He was a walking, talking, leading man in his own country noir. He was more cartoon than real. He was both a stereotype and completely unique. A grab bag of contradictions. An Ozarks original.

The next morning, Booger pulled up outside my motel room in a '67 bright red corvette stingray convertible. He was wearing cowboy boots and a Stetson hat. He wore jeans with a button-down, long-sleeved bright-ocean blue dress shirt, unbuttoned just enough at the top to show his thick, gold chain glistening out from beneath a dense crop of chest hair. He wore a thick leather belt with a buckle large enough to intrude into his oversized beer belly. He stood at least 6' 3" with a thick jaw and worn face. A small scar ran down his left cheek, and his eyes were dark.

For a cartoon, he made an intimidating presence. His arms were thick and leathered. His hands were the size of my face. My hand looked like a child's when he shook it the first time.

"You must be Alan," he said. "I'm Booger, Booger McLain.

"I hope you like your coffee thick and unfiltered," he said. "Hop in the car."

"Just a second," I replied. "Let me get my recorder and notepad."

"How's your memory, son?" he said with a grin.

"Fine, I guess."

"Good, 'cause I don't let anyone tape-record me, and you're not going to write down anything I tell you. Everything I say is off the record. Do you understand?"

"Yes, sir," I replied.

"Good, now get in the car."

He didn't say a word to me as we drove. The radio was turned up high and played country music and not the light country. He played Waylon Jennings, Johnny Cash and Hank Williams.

He pulled into the parking lot of Joe's Diner. It was a small place, about the size of a single-wide mobile home. Inside was a porcelain counter spanning most of the length of the diner. Opposite the counter, against the front glass windows that ran the length of the restaurant, were eight booths large enough to accommodate four individuals each.

The counter was completely full of customers, but only three of the booths were occupied. Booger led me to the booth at the very end, farthest away from other customers. He took the seat that placed his back against the wall.

"Old habit," he said. "I used to be a detective. They taught us to always sit at the end, back against the wall, so we had a good view of everything in front of us, and no one could sneak up from behind."

I didn't know what to think about Booger. I wasn't able to get a good read on him yet. Was this whole thing a con? Was he just toying with me, or did he intend to give me information that would shed some light on what happened a year earlier?

"Hey, Booger," a waitress from behind the counter shouted out just after we sat down. "Do you and your friend want any breakfast or just coffee?"

"Just coffee, honey." He replied.

"Just my luck today. Everyone's a big spender," she said back, carrying a pot of coffee and two coffee cups. "Who's your friend?" she asked, looking at me while she poured two cups of coffee.

"He's not a friend Rose. Just an admirer."

"Yeah, right," she replied in a sarcastic tone. "I don't

think it's possible for a cheap ass, grumpy old man like you to have an admirer."

"I didn't say me, Rose. He admires your voluptuous body and uplifting personality," Booger said with a smile.

"Watch it, kid," she replied. "The manure coming out of his mouth is gonna swallow you up if you're not careful."

I took a sip of the coffee and nearly choked. It was thick like oil. It sort of smelled and tasted like oil, or what I could imagine a quart of 20 weight tasting like.

"You OK, kid?" Booger asked when he saw me struggling to swallow. "Rose always gives me the bottom of the pot, the shit that's been sitting around the longest. She says it makes me more congenial. I think she loves me."

"Has anyone died drinking this?" I asked, reaching for a glass of water to get the taste out of my mouth.

"The coroner always rules the deaths a suicide," he said with a smirk. "So, what are you here to ask me, son?"

"I want to know what happened to Steve Raymond and Gary Walker."

"They drowned," he replied.

"No, I mean, what led up to their death? Do you think they were murdered?"

"It doesn't matter what I think. It only matters what I can prove, and I can't prove a damn thing yet."

"You must have an idea what happened?"

"Why do you want to know, son? From what I gather,

you have no connection to the family, you're not a real reporter, and you're not a cop. Why do you have any interest in what happened to those boys?"

"You're right. I wish that I didn't have an interest in what happened. But I do. For over a year, I've tried to forget about the day those bodies floated to the top of the lake. But I can't. I see them over and over again in my head. I was there that day, on campus. I saw those fully clothed bodies floating in the water. Every instinct that I had told me that those boys just didn't go for a swim and drowned. Nothing made sense to me. I assumed there would be an investigation. I assumed the police would do something."

"And you were wrong," Booger replied. "This is the Ozarks, son. We like to keep things quiet, peaceful. We like to leave things well enough alone, particularly when it involves locals. Have you ever heard the term, *hill justice?*"

"No."

"Well, hill people and by that, I mean most of the people that have lived their entire lives in the Ozarks, like to take care of their own problems. They are, for the most part, good, honest, hardworking folks that believe in an eye for an eye, that type of thing. If someone crosses them, they deal with it their own way. They don't have much use for the law, and for the most part, the law pretty much leaves them alone. Life is much easier when you don't wake a sleeping rattlesnake, if you know what I mean.

"If I was a betting man, I'd say those boys did more than wake a sleeping rattlesnake. Hell, they climbed into the nest with them. I'm not saying they got what they deserved, but whatever they did put them face to face with hill justice."

"Do you know what they did that was bad enough to get them killed?" I asked, with budding confidence.

"Wait a second, son. I didn't say they were killed. Don't put words in my mouth. Fact is, if anyone knows what happened to those two boys, they're sure as hell not talkin' 'bout it."

"But you've been investigating their deaths for nearly a year. You must have some idea what happened to them, what led up to their deaths."

"Listen to me, son. The Raymonds are good people. They're having trouble accepting the loss of their only child. They remember only the good in him and refuse to accept that he was capable of doing anything wrong. When they contacted me, I felt sorry for them. I wanted to help. I thought that I could help.

"Rose bring some more coffee," he yelled at the waitress without missing a beat before turning back to me. "They had gone to the police, but they refused to do anything. The boys' deaths had been ruled accidental drownings. I told them that I would look into the death of their son. I even took a retainer of $500 to investigate. Looking back on it now, I shouldn't have ever taken the case.

"I never thought those boy's deaths were accidental. My gut told me from the beginning they were murdered. But it doesn't matter what I think or what my gut tells me. It only matters what I can prove, and I can't prove a damn thing. I tried to tell Dorothy and Earl that. But they refused to listen. When my retainer ran out, I didn't ask for any more money. I didn't take it from them because I couldn't give them answers. I was never going to be able to give them answers.

"Earl had a stroke a few months back. Probably the stress. The frustration had nowhere to go except a bubble in his brain. After the stroke, he refused to even look at me when I'd stop by. He had lost hope. I still talk to Dorothy every now and then. She always asks how the investigation is going. So, what do I tell her? Exactly what she wants to hear: I'm still working leads, Darlin.' Nothing much to report right now, but it all can turn on a dime.' She knows better. She just doesn't want to."

"But you had to find out a few things during your investigation," I asked.

Booger sat there staring at me for several seconds. Then he raised his hand and motioned to Rose, who was serving customers at the counter. "Bring us a couple of those day-old do-nuts, doll," he said.

Then he sat back in the booth, pulled a cigar out of his pocket, bit off the tip and put it in his mouth. He grabbed a book of matches off the table and lit it up, taking a long, slow drag on it."

"Oh, shit," Rose said as she reached the table with two glazed do-nuts and more coffee. "When he takes out a stogie, it means he's planting his ass in that seat," she said, looking directly at me. "There goes my day. Any chance you might tip me by the cup rather than occupy my booth all day and leave me with a quarter, Booger?"

"Nah, but I can give you your quarter now if you want, Rose."

"No, you surprise me," she replied with a snarl.

"Notice I brought a fresh pot of coffee this time," she said, turning to me with what must have been a half smile. "With all your gagging, some of the other customers thought my coffee was killing was you."

"Thanks," I said as she quickly walked away.

"So, what did you find out during your investigation?" I asked the stetson-wearing detective.

"I found out that some of what Dorothy and Earl were saying about their son was true. For the most part, he was a good kid. He didn't drink in high school, and he didn't take drugs, as far as I could tell. He got good grades, was smart, and no one really had anything bad to say about him. He had a girlfriend. Dorothy probably told you about her. She thought of her as a daughter after her son's death. They were close for quite a while. It was a shame about the baby. Did she tell you about it?"

"Yeah, she said Steve never knew about the baby, that she aborted it without him knowing."

"Shit," Booger replied. "Dorothy is living in a fantasy world, believing only what she wants to believe. The abortion is a story that Becky Jacobs told her, so she didn't have to tell her what really happened."

"What really happened?" I asked.

"It was a car accident on one of those narrow country roads in the hills northwest of Branson. She never said what she was doing there. It was out in the middle of nowhere. She told the police that she had got lost. A truck pulled out in front of her off a dirt road. She swerved, and the car went down an embankment. She was pretty banged up and taken to a hospital. She lost the baby."

"Why didn't she tell the Raymond family the truth?"

"You'd have to ask her that," Booger replied. "But that might be a little difficult, seeing that she's buried in Riverside Cemetery."

"What?"

"Yeah, I'm sure Dorothy didn't tell you that, did she?" Booger replied.

"No, what happened to her?" I asked.

"Drug overdose," Booger replied. "Coroner said that she had a lethal dose of a substance similar to cocaine in her system. Odd thing to happen to her since no one I talked to was aware she ever tried drugs."

"What do you think?" I asked.

"I think drugs and car accidents are the two most common ways young folks die in the Ozarks."

"So, what do you really think happened to her?" I asked again.

Booger took another sip of coffee and another drag on his cigar.

"I think whoever was responsible for her boyfriend's death wasn't done doling out his brand of hill justice. Or," he added, "Maybe she was just another junkie that was also a terrible driver. Hell, son. I don't know, and assumptions are for asses."

For Booger, it seemed a turn of phrase was an art form, and speculation was for suckers. He only wanted to talk in facts or his own brand of sarcasm — the kind that built the plastic mystique of a chest-hair-bearing cowboy in a hot rod.

I resolved myself that day to not waste my time chasing his speculations. "Can you tell me about Gary Walker?" I asked.

"He had a tough life, grew up poor in a rundown mobile home. His dad was a drunk that went out for a drink one night and never came home. His mother was sickly. She worked odd jobs when she felt good enough, and Gary dropped out of high school to help make ends meet. He seemed like a good enough kid, maybe a little simple, maybe a little naïve, and maybe a little too trusting."

"He, for certain, had a poor choice in women. I believe his girlfriend's name was Rachael. She was a waitress at a dive bar called Billy Bobs — a favorite watering hole for workers and jerkers. She'd given herself to most of the regulars. When Gary began coming around, it might be she thought she had some fresh dog to walk around the block. She had boobs, I understand. She was experienced, which is a nice way of saying she had saggy boobs. Anyway, simple Gary fell in love with her, which makes a dog hard to get rid of. You take 'em to the park and let 'em go, but they just look at you with big dumb eyes and hop back in the pickup, grinning. I don't know what her plan was, but she held a tight grip on him. Maybe she wanted something."

"What do you think she wanted?" I asked.

"I suspect it was money. She had four children at home fathered by three ex-husbands, none of which was helping her support those kids. Her barmaid job didn't bring in much income. I think she was desperate and saw Gary as someone who could get her some money, with the right motivation, of course. That was when she came up with the plan to fake her pregnancy. She told him he was the father. From what I heard, he wanted to marry her. I don't think she expected that, and I know that wasn't what she wanted. Eventually, she was able to convince him that having her magic abortion was the best option, but Gary had to pay for it. 'Hey dog, get me that bone.' But simple Gary was poor and simple. He was still living at home in that worn-down trailer with his mother. He didn't have any money or a map to get it. That's when the next guy came into Rachael's life. This guy was more promising. He had some money. His name was Harley. He was a bad dude, recently out of prison for murder, and he hadn't exactly been law-abiding since he got out. He was a small-time drug dealer, from what I discovered. He ran a group of whores, too — street pros. Most were addicted to his drugs. I did not find they belonged to any local church choirs or college sororities if ya follow. I never did figure out what he saw in Rachael. Maybe he had plans for her to turn tricks for him, maybe bring up the quality of his street hookers just a bit.

"On the outside and from a little distance, I had been told by men that knew her she had long legs and enough make-up to look ten years younger in a dim light. She certainly, as I may have mentioned prior, had boobs. They'd get together almost every time Harley came to Springfield. I imagine only she knows just how or if she kept Gary from finding out. At some point, Harley trusted her enough or maybe was just drunk enough to share details of his business with her. It wasn't a lot that he shared, but it was enough to get her thinking.

"It is possible she saw Harley as another mark— someone she could use, take advantage of. A dangerous game, in my opinion. But Rachael was not the type of woman that got her own hands dirty when there was someone else available to do it for her. That's where Gary came in.

"But no plan is perfect, particularly when a combination of drugs and greed are the foundation for said plan. Harley had introduced her to a new type of drug, something called meth."

"Math?" I asked.

"Meth."

"Myth?"

"Meth!" he yelled this time in the small diner, pulling his cigar out of his mouth. Everyone stopped for a second and looked at us. Unphased, he gave a wand's wave of his stogie, and everyone returned to their diner activities.

"No one knows why he supplied her with it. Maybe he just wanted to make the sex that much better. Or, maybe he wanted to get her hooked. Or maybe she stole it away in her already crammed halter top. I don't like to speculate," he said, seeming very much to enjoy the speculation.

"Regardless, her time was running out. She was becoming more dependent on the drugs. She wasn't certain how long she could keep Harley a secret. Time was moving fast. Her belly would need to start showing a bump soon, or simple Gary could get suspicious. Her relationship with Harley was a tender box. She couldn't control him like a loyal dog. He was a wanderer, a completely unpredictable target. She had to act soon if she was going to pull off her biggest con."

He held a look with the last sentence for maximum impact.

"Rose, this poor skinny boy needs another one of those belly bomber do-nuts!"

CHAPTER 7
THE BIG ASK

Rachael moved her hand slowly, gently to the bulge in his pants. She moved her lips close to his, just inches away. Her seductive smile and the touch of her hand aroused him. She had a unique hold on Gary. Excited, he leaned in towards her. She backed off. Rachael was toying with him. He was a meal. She was preparing to devour him.

She hadn't seen Gary in nearly two weeks. She had avoided him, aiming to make him desperate for her attention.

"I wasn't sure I would see you again," he said.

"I needed some time to think," she replied.

"I love you, Rachael," he said in a soft voice. It was the first time he had told her that.

"I love you too, Gary. But I'm not sure that I can depend

on you."

"Of course, you can. I would do anything for you," he said, confused. "Marry me. I'll take care of you and our baby."

She turned stern suddenly. "Damn, Gary. That's just what I mean. Marriage is just not realistic right now. I have four kids at home, four mouths to feed and clothe. My job barely pays the bills. You don't have any money. You are barely making it, and you know it's true. How in the hell are you going to support me, my kids and a new baby?"

He closed his mouth, which was ready to answer before she cut him off at the pass. He didn't know how he'd support her. His eyes turned down. He was defeated.

"Gary, the only answer right now is an abortion. I checked into the cost. I think it's going to be around $2,000, maybe more. Do you have that kind of money?"

"No," he replied softly.

"Do you have any clue how to get that kind of money?"

"No. But I have been thinkin'. I can quit school and maybe get a full-time job at the 3M plant. I know they're hiring. Maybe one of the guys at the bar…."

"Gary, I need the abortion now," she interrupted, "not in two or three months or however long it takes you to earn what I need with a good job." She paused and then switched gears to a softer tone. She was shifting into second to round a corner. "Do you have any relatives or friends that can loan you the money?"

"No."

Jumping straight into fourth gear, "Damn, Gary, you're useless," and she turned away from him.

"Don't say that, Rachael. I love you," he said, feeling desperate. "I'll find a way to get it."

Rachael smiled just a little. The corners of her mouth didn't flinch, but her lips tightened slightly as if she needed to hold a paper clip between them. With her back to him, he never saw it.

Rachael's voice now went waitress-sweet. "Oh, Gary." Her face was plastic. Everything from here was a show. She knew what she had to say and quickly thought about her ten-year anniversary at Billy Bob's when she dropped that tray of two pitchers just after her C-section with little Tommy. Her boss yelled that he would dock her check —' and he did. She wasn't even supposed to be back to work yet. She was devasted. It was a feeling that was never too far away. That was when she let go of her childhood dream to become a dancer. Only a couple of people had ever known about her dream and how she had built it up and protected it, even against great odds. When she let it die, no one knew, but she knew. She'd lock the pain away because it was too much to bear. In time, she realized she could use it whenever she wanted. Her pain, saved away, was a weapon. And it was bottomless. Standing next to Gary, her eyes welled up, and she turned back to him. "I may have a way for you to get the money we need."

"What? Anything," he said with fresh hope, ready to answer the call.

"There is a guy who comes into the bar once in a while. He's a creep, an older guy, a drunk. He makes passes at me. I can't stand to look at him."

Rachael could see the jealousy, the anger building on Gary's face. "He's tried to get me to go out with him. He has no idea how much he disgusts me. He thinks he's God's gift to women. He's just like a hundred guys I've met before. He, like the others, just wants to get in a girl's pants. They look at all women as pieces of meat to be used and disposed of. Sometimes I hate my job. I need to be nice to all the creeps regardless of how much I hate it."

"What's his name? I'll beat the shit out of him," Gary responded earnestly.

"His name is Harley. But calm down for a minute because I have more to tell you.," she said. "Harley drinks a lot, and the more he drinks, the more he talks. At first, I thought he was just bragging about all the money he had. I told him he was full of shit and that he probably didn't have a pot to piss in. That's when he pulled out a wad of cash. It was a wad of hundred-dollar bills about four inches thick. I can't even imagine how much money it was. He said it was about $10,000. Maybe it was, maybe it wasn't. I had no way of knowing. But I know that I have never seen that much money before. He said that he had a lot more, that he was rich.

"I didn't believe him, of course. Men say anything when they just want, you know," taking an extra second to say it, "to use you."

She saw a change in Gary's expression, a bit of a shocked look like he didn't expect a statement like that from her.

"Oh, I didn't mean you, Gary," she said, amused. "You're not like most men. You're kind and considerate. You would never use a woman like some men do."

Gary's face relaxed, and she continued.

"Like I said, I didn't really believe he was wealthy, but I did see that wad of cash. Now, Gary, promise me you won't get angry or get too upset over what I'm going to tell you."

"I promise," he said with a concerned look.

"Harley said he would give me the entire wad of cash, all $10,000, if I would spend the night with him."

Rachael watched as his neck, then his face turned red with anger. "I'll kill the son of a bitch," he yelled back.

"No, you promised me you wouldn't get angry, Gary. He was drunk. Guys say and do a lot of crazy shit when they're drunk. There was no fucking way I was going to sleep with him, not for any amount of money. Gary, I love you. I don't give a shit about him. Like I said, he disgusts me."

She moved her lips close to him and kissed him gently on the cheek to calm him. She was a fly, tucking him in a warm web blanket.

"I was angry that night, too," she said in a serious, straightforward tone. "When I went home and went to bed, I started thinking about what he said. We need the money, Gary. There is no doubt about that. Ten thousand dollars would solve most of our troubles."

Now speaking faster so he couldn't interrupt: "Once I got the abortion, and we had a little nest egg left over, we could start making plans about our future. I love you, Gary, and I know you love me. That money would be enough to give us a fresh start."

"No, there is no fucking way I'm going to let you sleep with that creep to get the money. I'll find some other way," he replied, shaking, with tears in his eyes now.

"Listen to me, Gary. That's not what I meant. I wouldn't sleep with that old man for any amount of money. But there might be another way to get our hands on the cash."

"What do you mean?"

"I mean, all he has to think is that I am going to meet up with him, that I'm going to sleep with him. When he shows up, we can simply take his money. You know, maybe make it look like a robbery."

"Oh, Rachael. I don't know," he said, flustered by the pace of it all. "I've never robbed anyone. I don't know if I could do it. Besides, he'd call the police, I'm sure. They'd arrest me and you, too."

"No, you're not seeing the whole picture, Gary. There's no way he'll report it to the police. What would he say that he propositioned a girl and she took his money. That sounds a lot like him soliciting someone for prostitution. Hell, he'd be in trouble, too.

"There is something else, Gary, another reason he wouldn't call the cops. He told me how he got that much cash. He sells drugs. He's small-time, mind you, but he has some customers in Springfield that he sells to. When he comes in Billy Bobs, it is after he's collected the money. So, you see, he couldn't report the crime because the money he would have lost was money he got from selling drugs."

"Damn, I don't know. I don't know, Rachael. A guy who sells drugs is probably carrying a gun, and even if he isn't and suppose the robbery goes on without a hitch, he's going to be pissed. He's going to want his money back. He's going to come after me if he knows or worse, after you, Rachael. He'll figure you stole the money or set him up. Oh, I just don't know. I gotta feeling, and it ain't good."

"That's why he can never know I was involved. That's all. Drug dealers probably get robbed all the time. You've just got to make it look like a random robbery. He shows off his wads of cash all the time in the bar. I told him before that he shouldn't do that. Someone might get tempted to take it away from him. There are all kinds of characters that come in Billy Bob's. If we do things right, he'll think it was a stranger who knew he carried the money and decided to take it away from him. He'll blame himself. Or at least someone he's been bragging to. He's not going to think it's the girl he was going to pay for sex. You can see that, right?"

She was making him think. She was guiding him, giving him the answer. But it all felt wrong to Gary.

"How do we convince him, though? How can we be sure he won't blame you? I just don't want him thinking you might have set him up, right?

"You've got to rob us both, and you've got to hurt me."

This was the moment. This was the big ask. Gary was stunned, sickened.

"No, I've never beat up anyone before, and I sure as hell can't hurt you," he said timidly. He was serious, and he was scared.

"You've got to Gary. Otherwise, the plan just won't work. This is what it takes. This will convince him. He'll never think I had anything to do with it if I get hurt. Don't you understand? This is our chance. We won't have to worry about me, love. Just give a big smack and a couple bruises. I'll heal quick, and I don't mind. I want you to. I'm asking you to. For me. For us. What we need to worry about is you, Gary. I love you, Gary. We can do this, but you'll have to stay safe for me. Can you get your hands on a gun?"

"Oh no, I'm not going to shoot anybody," he said, tense, eyes wide on Rachael.

"No, of course not, but pointing the barrel of a gun at someone certainly gets their attention. You don't want him to fight back, do you?"

"No."

"Then you need a gun. It's simple. I'll help you through this. You just have to listen to me. I've been thinking this through. Do you know where to get one?"

"Yes, I think so. My father used to keep a handgun in the trailer for protection. I only knew him to use it once. That was to kill a snake that had crawled up underneath the porch."

"Well, get it. You'll need to bring it with you."

"What am I supposed to do with it?"

"You just do exactly what I say. You tell him to give you his money, that you won't hurt him or me if he does what you say. After he hands it to you, order him down on the ground, facing down. You have to talk like a boss. Like a general in the Army. Have him put his hands behind his back, then tie up his hands and legs like a calf. I know how good you are with knots. Remember that time we played that sex game. You tied my hands and feet so good. There was no way I could get free without your help. Tie him up the same way. And, speaking of, you'll need to bring some thick rope."

He nodded instinctively. He had learned how to tie knots in Boy Scouts to earn a merit badge, and there are some things you never forget.

"You'll need a ski mask, too, so he doesn't get a good look at you. After you've tied him up, empty his pockets. That's where the wad of cash will be. Also, be sure to check his motorcycle on the way out. He has a satchel tied to it. Take it. There might be some more cash or something else worthwhile in it. After you rob him, order me to hand over my jewelry and purse. I'll resist a little bit to make it seem genuine. That's when you slap me. And do it hard. You might have to shake me by the shoulders at first. I'll fall to the ground crying when you strike me, and you tie me up just the same as Harley. Take my jewelry and the money from my purse. All you need to do after that is leave quick."

"I can take you with me," he said. "I don't want to leave you alone with him."

"You've got to. He's got to believe I wasn't part of the plan, remember? He's got to believe you're just robbing us like what drug dealers and thieves do. I'll be fine. Once you leave and we're free, I'll be hysterical. He'll think that I'm as much of a victim as he is. And I'll make sure he gets good and drunk, so he won't have time to think when you pull the gun on him. There won't even be a fight. If he's acting wrong, I'll tell him we need to be cool. Once the ropes are on him, he can't do nothing, and you can do that quick. Gary, if we both play our parts right, he won't ever suspect we were in this together."

Rachael kissed Gary's cheek gently but intently as if

it was settled now, and there was nothing further to discuss. This was how it had to be. Gary was stunned and silent.

"After we get the money is going to be the most difficult part of it all," she said. "We're going to need to go a while without seeing each other. Harley doesn't know about you, but we'll need to be careful. No matter how good of an acting job we do, he might suspect it was someone who knew me, who knew we were meeting up for sex when he had that money," she said. Gary bristled at the word sex. In all the planning, he'd forgotten she'd be pretending to want Harley. She saw Gary's reaction but pressed on. "He'll probably watch me for a while to see if I spend time with anyone."

"How long do we need to stay apart?"

"Probably a couple of months. That means no phone calls, no stopping by the trailer, and no contact of any kind. And you know you can't say anything to anyone, or Harley could kill us both."

"I understand," he said, not really understanding. "But I don't like it. Is there another way?"

Rachael ignored him. "Good, you know we're doing this for both of us. After everything has settled, and after my abortion, we can be together again. We'll be able to start over. We can get married if you want."

And like that, he was sold. He already knew he couldn't tell her no, but now he was invested.

"Just do what you said, right?"

"Right. I'm going to have Harley meet me at the Wilson's Hollar."

Wilson's Hollar was a piece of country in the city, not far from downtown, on the west side, with a swimming hole —' an off-shoot of Wilson's Creek —' and an abundance of privacy, especially in the dark. Depending on who you talked to, it sprawled over several miles in between industrial sites, busy intersections and poorer, older neighborhoods. It included the grounds of an old, abandoned grain mill dating back to the 1800s, plenty of shadowy, dense brush, loose trash, feral cats and flood-water ditches. This was a playground for people who wanted to hide in plain sight. The creek connected to a popular northside park, Grant Beach Park. And all along it were hidden low places — perfect for brave secret lovers or robbing drug dealers.

"No one will be there but us," Rachael said, speaking of where they'd rendezvoused before. "And you can wait in the bushes just past the fences."

Gary flinched at this. This was where he'd first made love to Rachael. "What about the money? How do I get it to you so you can get the abortion?"

"I've thought about that. I figure Harley or maybe someone he knows will be watching me, but they won't think anything of me meeting up with a woman. Do you know a girl you can trust, maybe someone completely innocent, someone who has no idea what she is carrying, to drop the money off at my home?

"It could be wrapped like a gift, maybe, something that she was just dropping off as a favor."

"I don't really know anyone," Gary replied.

"Think, Gary. You must know someone that could drop a gift off. The barmaids I know would just give me something at work."

For a few seconds, he was quiet. Then a small smile came across his face.

"Maybe, I do. A good friend of mine has a girlfriend, well at least she used to be his girlfriend who lives not far from you. I think if I asked him to ask her, he would."

"Alright then. Ask him. Have him meet with her. Make him believe that you've broken up with me, that I'm seeing someone else, someone that is extremely jealous. Tell him you want to get some personal items back to me, but a man can't be seen going to my home. Get him to ask his girlfriend to drop a package off for you at my house. That way, only we know. If we wait until two days after, that should be enough. Tell me you can do that, Gary."

"Yes. Yes, I think so."

Now, she grabbed him and kissed him hard. She had worn her white, silky blouse—the one she wore when she needed things from men. He could feel her nipples pressed against his chest.

She guided him. Even now, she guided his seduction.

He was still now. He was warm. He was hers. The spider had swallowed the fly.

CHAPTER 8
DINER DRAMA

"Rose, can you bring us some more coffee?" Booger shouted from his corner seat.

"Damn it, Booger. We're going to have to start charging you rent for that booth. Don't you want some food? Some pie? Debbie made a fresh blueberry this morning."

"Nah, I gave up eating anything blue a long time ago. Turns my poops purple.

"But you can ask my friend. He's a city boy. I don't think he cares what his shit looks like."

"Son, do you want some blueberry pie or maybe something else?" Rose asked as she poured the coffee."

"No, I'm fine," I said, feeling a bit uncomfortable, like I was stuck between a war of wills. "I will take a little more water, though."

"Sure thing, hun. By the way, what are you doing with an old geezer like Booger, anyway?"

"I'm his protégé," Booger answered, pronounced pro-duh-gee, before I could respond. "He's here to learn as much wisdom as his brain can soak up. I'm a fountain, and he's a towel. Wish the kid luck."

We shared a glance when he said fountain. It seemed he surprised himself with his own special clever nonsense.

"Damn, the manure's getting deep in here," Rose replied before walking away.

"That woman loves me, son," Booger said to me once she was gone. "It's the McLain family charm. Sometimes it can be a curse."

"So, tell me, Booger. What went wrong with Rachael's plan?"

"A better question is, what went right? She was the brains of the operation, and I think that was the first problem. Rachael was no doubt accomplished at breasts presentation and making suckers outta suckers, but she wasn't half as smart as she thought she was. Rachael never made it past the tenth grade. That's when she got pregnant for the first time. Her entire life consisted of a series of poor choices. Hell, if there was a fork in the road with a sign pointing in one direction that read "right way" and another sign pointing in the other direction that said "also, the right way," she would go directly between them and plow into a tree."

Booger had used the fork-in-the-road line before.

"Everything that woman got involved in was destined to crash and burn. If I was a sigh-call-o-gist, I'd say she self-sabotaged everything.

"The other problem was Gary," Booger noted. "He was simple, as I've said. A good boy, I believe. The simples are the best people among us. It's the complicated people you've gotta worry about. His biggest mistake was getting involved with Rachael," Booger continued. "His second biggest mistake was listening to her. He really believed she knew what she was doing and that her plan would work. Poor boy was naïve. At first, it seems everything went as planned. Harley came into the bar at his usual time, late that Friday night. He sat at the bar in his usual spot and ordered draft beers with whiskey chaser as he always had before. There was something different about him that night, though, something Rachael didn't notice at first. He seemed anxious and nervous. He kept looking in the mirror over the bar. It reflected back toward the entrance. He was drunk quicker and faster than normal too. A customer who was sitting at the bar two barstools away from him told me Harley was quieter than normal. And he was the loud drunk type. There was something else, too, he said. Harley kept reaching down for his pocket. Once when he was doing it, the man says he'd swear he saw the handle of a gun sticking out of the edge.

"Rachael should have sensed something was wrong, but if she did, Harley's behavior wasn't off enough to - stop - the train once it left the station. A few minutes before closing time, Rachael began her move. She touched him gently, looked into his eyes and whispered in his ear that she wanted him that night. Several customers said Harley was completely shit-faced. He could barely get off the barstool, and Rachael had to help him walk outside. He was so drunk that he couldn't drive his motorcycle. Rachael drove. Harley held onto her waist as she sped off.

"From that point, it is purely speculation where they went for the next couple of hours. I do know that around 4 a.m., a passerby spotted Harley's motorcycle in a parking lot off of Grant Beach Park, adjacent to Wilson's Hollar, close to downtown and even closer to Rachael's home.

"Most of what happened there, I gathered from police reports and a handful of witnesses that were in the area. A white pick-up truck, an older model, pulled into the parking space next to Harley's motorcycle. A short time later, a cab pulled into the same parking lot. Gary got out of it. It seems that Gary's car wouldn't start, so, in desperation, he called a cab to take him to the park.

"The cab driver remembered him because of how nervous he was. He also reeked of beer. The driver kept an eye on him from the rearview window the entire way to Grant's Beach. He was afraid the kid would either try to rob him or upchuck in his back seat."

"I don't mean to interrupt, Booger," I said. "But who was driving the white pick-up truck?"

"There were actually two guys. We know from a witness who saw them leaving the park in the truck, but the details were slim. They only could say for sure the boys burned rubber when they left and sported baseball caps. Like I said, slim."

"So, what happened in the park, Booger?"

"Well, that's a little foggy. There were no witnesses to exactly what happened there except for the ones that were directly involved. Rachael knew what happened. So did Gary and those two men in the pick-up truck knew. Harley probably knew some of what happened. But obviously, he didn't know everything.

"The witnesses that were there can't speak about it anymore, is what we know. One can speculate about some of what happened based on the people I interviewed and the evidence I found.

"We know Rachael and Harley got there first. She took him back into the park to a wooded area where they had made love before. From other accounts, Harley seemed too drunk to get it up, so I doubt they had sex. I think Rachael probably spent that time just trying to keep Harley conscious enough to understand he was being robbed for when simple Gary showed up. If the plan was for them to rob Harley naked in the woods, a suspicious cab driver didn't help. Stumbling, sleepy Harley with a six-shooter didn't help. And two ballcap boys definitely didn't help.

"These ballcap boys are a key here. The wad of cash Harley was carrying and the drugs that were thought to be on him were gone when the police arrived. We know people heard gunfire coming from the park. That's when people close by called the police. A man out for an early morning jog saw a woman covered in blood running out of the park with a young man. Sounds like Rachael and simple, drunk Gary to me. Another cab driver who picked up the two of them said the woman, a middle-aged lady with heavy make-up, was hysterical. She had several large spots of blood on her white blouse. The man was much younger, maybe college-age. He seemed to be trying to calm her down but was visibly shaken himself. The cabbie dropped both of them off just six blocks away in a residential neighborhood. The place the cab driver dropped them off happened to be less than a block from Rachael's house.

"When the police arrived at the park, they found Harley lying on the ground in a pool of blood. He had been shot three times. An ambulance arrived soon after and rushed him to the hospital. Miraculously, he would survive. The bullets that lodged inside him came from a small caliber revolver, similar to the one that Gary took from his mother's trailer and was thought to have brought with him into the park that night."

Booger sat back in the booth. Took another cigar out of his pocket, lit it up and took several long drags. Then, he looked over at Rose. She was behind the counter cleaning up. The diner was nearly empty now. The lunch crowd had left, and the dinner crowd hadn't arrived yet.

"Can you bring us more coffee, darling?" he said.

"If you call me darling again, I'm going to serve this pot of coffee right in your lap."

"See, I told you, son. She wants my bod, always coming up with excuses to warm my crotch."

"You sure you don't want to switch to decaf?" she asked, looking directly at Booger. "I think the caffeine has gone to your brain, old man."

"No, only to my heart, love. You know there's no other woman in the world for me other than you, Rose."

"That's only because there's no other woman in the world that would put up with you," she replied.

"Kid," she said, looking directly at me with a bit of a smile, "Don't listen to this old codger. Every word that comes out of his mouth is made up of three parts grade-A manure and one part dime store perfume to cover up the stench."

After Rose walked away, I asked Booger, "Did the police ever talk to Rachael or Gary?"

"Yeah, I believe it was two days later. Like I said earlier, neither were the sharpest knives in the drawer. Gary, in a hurry to get him and Rachael out of the park, dropped the gun that he had brought. It was recovered by the police early that morning. Rachael didn't exactly cover her tracks, either. Her romance with Harley was no secret. Just about everybody that spent any time in Billy Bob's knew about it. Hell, the only person acquainted with either of them who didn't know was simple Gary.

"The police didn't need to work very hard to determine Rachael and Gary were in the park that night for reasons that did not include sharing the Good News about Jesus. They brought both of them in at the same time and interrogated them in different rooms. Classic police move. Of course, they told completely different stories. All of that should have been predictable to more clever folk. They had two days to come up with one story, and all they could offer were half-truths.

"Gary said he went to the park because Rachael had called him and asked him to meet her there, that she wanted to talk about the baby. Rachael's story was she went to the park with Harley to break up with him. Confronted with evidence that neither story was truthful and threatened with arrest, both Rachael and Gary confessed to their real intentions in the park that night: to rob Harley. But two masked men got to him first, they said. Gary, as it was told, only reached Rachael after the two men had left. During the course of the robbery, one of the men, the taller one, according to Rachael, shot Harley three times. Then they ran off. Rachael was hysterical by the time Gary arrived. She was only inches away from Harley when he was shot. Blood splattered on her face, blouse and skirt. They both thought Harley was dead. Their only thoughts were to get out of that park and get home as soon as possible. They spotted an on-duty cab just outside the park that had just dropped a worker off at a restaurant across from the park. The cab driver took them just near Rachael's house. She said she chose not to have the cab driver drop her off at her house because she could tell he was 'suspicious' and might report them to the police. You know, the girl was covered in blood.

"Gary didn't realize his gun was missing until later that day. That's when he returned to the park to try to find it. But the police were still there, and yellow police tape had been strung up around the area. The police let both of them go. They had no evidence that a crime had been committed by either of them other than Gary carrying a concealed weapon, and hell, if they were going to arrest him for that, they'd have to arrest a quarter of the residents of Springfield. This is God-fearing, gun-toting land."

I looked at Booger. He seemed to be lost in his thoughts for a second. "So, did Harley shed any light on what happened that night? Did he know who the men were that robbed him?"

"Harley went through surgery early that morning. When he came out, the doctors weren't certain he would pull through. The bullets didn't strike any vital arteries, but he had lost a lot of blood, and they were worried about infection. So, he was put into a medically induced coma for the next three days. It was nearly a week before the police could talk to him. When they did, he had little to say. He couldn't remember who shot him. He denied that he was robbed of anything. In fact, he denied that he was carrying any money at all. He even told them he had no idea how he got to the park or why he was there. He said his memory of that night was completely blank."

"Do you think he knew what happened to him?" I asked.

"I think he thought he knew, which is why I suspect things went the way they did after he got out of the hospital. We know that soon after he was released from the hospital, he sent a message to Rachael."

"What was the message?"

"Her house was burned down. It was the middle of the night. She had recently got off work and had just fallen asleep. Her two youngest children were asleep in her bed too. The older two children were asleep in their room. It was a tiny house, with only two bedrooms, a small living room, kitchen and one bathroom. The fire was started in the living room. An accelerant was used, gasoline, the arson investigator reasoned. The fire spread quickly, barely enough time for Rachael and her four children to escape through a bedroom window."

"Did the police suspect Harley of the fire?" I asked.

"No, in fact, they suspected that either Rachael or Gary

plotted to burn down the house."

"Why?" I asked.

"Well, Rachael was suspected because the police discovered she was desperate for money. Her mortgage hadn't been paid in months. Her bills were piling up, and collection agencies were dogging her. Remember, she had confessed she had gone to the park with Harley with the intention of robbing him. They thought the fire was a desperate attempt to get insurance money that would resolve her financial problems."

"But why was Gary suspected?" I asked.

"The police discovered that Rachael had lied about her pregnancy. She had strung Gary along, thinking he was the father in hopes that he would come up with the money. That idea was supported by an associate at Billy Bob's she had confided in. Plus, the police knew she was desperate for money. They suspected Gary found out about the false pregnancy and became aware of the con, aware of Rachael using him. There was little doubt the boy had fallen in love with her and thought she loved him too. Imagine how he would have felt when he found out that everything he believed, everything he thought would happen in his relationship with Rachael, was false. That's a recipe for revenge, and so the cops thought they were onto something. In the absence of the obvious, the police seeking a motive. Gary should have had a lot of that."

"So, what did the police do?" I asked.

"Well, they brought both of them in and questioned

them separately and at different times. But both denied any involvement. By this time, the police station was becoming their home away from home. Rachael, naturally, expressed outrage and indignation at being accused of burning her own house down and jeopardizing her kiddos. Gary seemed dumbfounded. He was genuinely shocked when he heard that Rachael's pregnancy was a lie. In fact, he broke down in tears at the news. In addition, Gary provided an alibi. He said he spent that night drinking beers with his best friend, Steve Raymond. He said they went to Rockaway Beach, a resort area near Branson and drank most of the night. They were too drunk to drive back to Nixa, so they spent the night there, sleeping on the ground near the lake."

"The police interviewed buddy Steve shortly thereafter. He confirmed Gary's story."

"So, where did that leave the arson investigation?" I asked.

"Pretty much dead in the water. The detective assigned to the case continued to suspect Rachael was the one that started the fire, so much so that he got the Department of Child Protective Services involved. A few days later, a court order was signed, and social workers accompanied by police showed up at Gary's trailer, where Rachael and her children had been staying since the fire. They took the children away that day."

"Wait," I said, struggling to understand what Booger

had just said. "So, Rachael and her kids were living in Gary's mother's mobile home, even after Gary realized her pregnancy was fake and she was only using him to get money?"

"Ain't love grand?" Booger said with a knowing smile. "I'm telling you, the boy was several fries shy of a happy meal. Poor Gary. The halter tops had a hold on his soul. They have a mystifying effect. They can wipe out reason."

Booger stared off for a moment. It was long enough that I started to look out the window to see what he was seeing.

"Anyways, he remained in love with her," he said, snapping back, "and it didn't seem anything she did was going to change that. So, after the fire, he moved her and her kids into that tiny, run-down mobile home that he shared with his sickly mother. I can only imagine what his mother thought. She was confined to her bed then. Hell, she couldn't even go to the bathroom without help. There were only two bedrooms. His mother had one, and Gary, Rachael and her four kids slept in the other bedroom. It must have been one cozy little family.

"Rachael continued to work at Billy Bobs. There was only one car, an old beat-up Chevy. Gary would drive the twenty miles every night to take Rachael to work and then would drive back after the bar closed to pick her up. God only knows what the kids did with sick Grandma when both of them were gone.

"Anyway, the police couldn't prove she started the

fire, but given the circumstances, Social Services felt there was enough evidence Rachael had endangered the kiddos, so they picked them up about two weeks after the fire. And the story's not done there. The day the kids were taken, Rachael showed up at work at her normal time, and a letter was waiting for her. It had been left with the bartender earlier in the day by an older, scraggly-looking man the bartender had never seen before. The letter was folded into a plain white envelope, and on the outside, it was addressed to Rachael."

"What did the note say?" I asked.

"That, no one knows for sure. It was sealed, and to my knowledge, no one other than Rachael and, likely, Gary read the contents. We can assume that whatever was in that letter sent the rest of what happened into motion.

"Rachael opened the letter at the bar. When she finished reading it, she put it in her purse, told the bar manager that she wasn't feeling well and left." Booger continued. "She was visibly upset," both the bar manager and the bartender told police later. "We know that she called Gary just before she left the bar. Witnesses heard her on the phone with him. Not long after she went outside, he drove up, and she got in his car. Then he drove off with her in the passenger seat.

"It was two days later that Gary called the police. He was frantic. Rachael had disappeared. She didn't leave a note. She didn't say anything to him. She just disappeared. Gary told the police he was certain that Harley had something to do with her disappearance. They attempted to contact Harley. The name and contact information that he provided them was false."

Booger took another sip of coffee, then sat back in his seat and smiled just a little. "Small-town cops, you've got to love 'em," he said. "They never thought to follow up on the information he gave them until after Rachael disappeared. Had they just gotten his fingerprints, they would have discovered his criminal background, his time in prison and that his real name wasn't Harley at all. His name was Michael Malott.

"But it wasn't just the police that was conned by him. The hospital where he stayed never checked to see if the information he gave them was accurate. The people in Billy Bob's bar who talked to him, that knew him and befriended him, never thought to ask if he had a name other than Harley. That was supposedly the name he was given because he was always known to ride a Harley Davidson motorcycle. If anyone the police talked to ever bothered to ask his real name, nobody would admit it, or maybe they didn't remember the name he provided them."

"Well, I've got to ask you, Booger, how did the police discover his real name?"

"I told them," he replied.

"What?" I asked.

"Yeah, I told them. Well, I didn't exactly tell them,

I guess. I just gave them the information they needed to discover his real name. You see, he and I sort of met shortly after I started working for the Raymond family. It was what you would probably call a chance meeting.

"But a lot had happened before I got involved in the case, before the Raymonds hired me, before I was nearly murdered."

CHAPTER 9
LOVE LOST AND FOUND

Rachael jumped into the passenger side of Gary's car. She was sobbing uncontrollably at first. It was a miserable night. The rain was pounding down on the beat-up two-door Gremlin. The windshield wipers were on high, and they were barely helping. Visibility came in the flashes between the blades. Thunder roared, and lightning illuminated the dark, dense clouds causing a haze that glistened through the windshield. Gary gripped the steering wheel tight and squinted and leaned forward to see.

He tried to comfort Rachael as best he could, resting his right hand on top of her leg when he could manage fleeting free moments to guide the steering wheel with his left. She was too upset to talk, still managing an overflow of tears, belches of whimpers, sinus drain and gasps for air. The fuss was indistinguishable from the storm. Gary was in survival mode, fixed on getting her back to the trailer as soon as he could. Perhaps, he thought, being home with a couple of shots of whiskey might calm her down enough for him to understand what had gone so terribly wrong.

Whiskey was never Rachael's choice of drink. She almost exclusively drank beer. Maybe a glass of wine once in a while. Sometimes a brandy if she was struggling to sleep, but almost never whiskey.

But that night, she needed her senses dulled as quickly as possible. Her body was trembling. She couldn't stop crying. Gary had never seen her like that before. So, she drank whiskey, Southern Comfort 100 proof. Gary had bought a quart of it a couple of weeks earlier. He had seen it advertised. It sounded like something he might like. It was not. It was too strong for him, with an odd combination of sweetness and bitterness that burned his throat and left an aftertaste that reminded him of siphoned gas.

The bottle was nearly full when he gave Rachael the first drink. Twenty minutes later, it was half empty. That was when Rachael told Gary about the letter.

"It was from Harley," she said. "He thinks we were the ones that shot him and took his money and drugs. He didn't outright say it, but he eluded to the fire that burned down my house. I know he was the person that set it."

"Does he know about me, Rachael?" Gary asked.

"Yeah, he knows about you. I don't know how, but he does. He thinks you and I were in on a plan to kill him and take everything he had.

"He said he'd come after you, and more bad things would happen to me if we didn't come up with $40,000 within the next two days. He included a map of the place where we need to drop off the money. It's down in the Ozarks, in hill country, secluded and not close to any town.

"I'm scared, Gary. I don't know what to do."

Gary put his head down into his hands. He was scared too. He needed time to think. His entire life had always been a struggle, but he had never faced a situation like this. He barely had enough money to pay for his next meal. There was no way he could come up with $40,000, not in a year, let alone two days.

"Do you think we could talk to him, maybe get him to understand that we had nothing to do with the robbery?" Gary asked.

Rachael's demeanor changed. She was angry and disappointed, as if she had just suddenly realized she was dealing with a child. "What the fuck, Gary? What do you think he'll do to us if we tell him that? Say he believes us? That everything is forgiven? Maybe, send us home with a hug and warm wishes?

"Damn it, Gary. This isn't a fucking game. He burned

down my house, for damn sake, with me and my children in it. I think he's pretty fucking serious, don't you?"

"Yeah, you're probably right. But we could tell him about the two men that were the ones that actually shot him and then robbed him. The police talked to people that saw them. There was even a newspaper article that speculated that they were the ones that committed the crime."

"I swear, Gary. I think you have shit for brains. The police think we're the ones that shot and robbed Harley. Hell, you even left your fucking gun at the scene of the crime. You know what the police think, don't you? They think that if those two men did shoot and rob Harley, that you and I must have got them to do it. No way who sliced this turd pie. We're the ones that are going to get blamed for eating it."

Gary took another sip of whiskey, then thought for a few seconds before speaking. "OK, suppose we ask for more time to come up with the money? What do you think he'd do?"

"He's a fucking psychopath Gary. How do you think he'd react?"

"Well, we need to try something. There is no way we can come up with that kind of money. What about the insurance on your house, Rachael?"

"Gary," she responded in a soft tone, much like an adult trying to explain to a child something that is beyond their comprehension. "The arson investigator thinks we are the ones that burned down my house. We're lucky that we haven't been arrested for that yet. No insurance company is going to pay off on a house fire that has been ruled arson, particularly when the owner of that house is the main suspect in starting the fire.

"Damn, Gary. I need some crank. That crap liquor you gave me is barely giving me a buzz, and it's not doing anything for my shakes. I don't suppose any of your redneck buddies knows where I can find a supply."

"Nah, I was out a while back with some guys that had a little weed, but I don't really know them."

"Weed won't do it for me, Gary."

"What do we do, Rachael?"

"Let me put it to you this way: Harley's pissed at me, but you're the one he wants to kill. I think what you should be asking yourself is, what are you going to do to get us out of this mess?"

"Damn, Rachael, this whole thing was your idea. You're the one that wanted to rob Harley. He's going to blame you as much as me."

"Really?" Rachael was exasperated. She took another shot of whiskey. "Let me paint a picture for you. I was dating Harley. Surprised? Yeah, I bet you are. You're so fucking naïve. Hell, I got news for you, we were fucking, and you know what, he's a real man. He knows how to please a woman. We'd been seeing each other behind your back, hell right under your nose, for weeks, late at night, in the same place, the park where we were the night he was attacked.

"Follow me because I know this is a little hard for you to understand. But he loved me. It wouldn't be hard for him to believe that my jealous ex-boyfriend found out about us, followed us to the park and, in a fit of rage, shot him and then stole his money and drugs. Damn, Gary. You even dropped your gun in the park.

"If I wanted to. All that I'd need to do is tell him that story. Yeah, he'd be pissed at me, might even beat the shit out of me, but he'd kill your ass."

Gary was stunned. He'd never seen her so angry, so mean. None of it made sense to him. "What about our baby, Rachael? Did he know that you were pregnant with my baby?"

"Remember, I wasn't pregnant, dumb shit. The police told you that I was using you. God, you are so fucking simple. I needed some money. I figured you could help. I didn't count on you being totally worthless. Hell, I'm a fuck'n magnet for losers."

Gary looked like someone that had just been hit in the gut with a two-by-four. Rachael wasn't the girl he knew. He didn't understand what was happening. He couldn't process it all so fast. He felt sick.

"I can't believe you cheated on me, and I can't believe you lied to me about the baby. I would have married you. Rachael. I love you."

"Damn, Gary. I tell you that a psychopath wants to kill you, and all you care about is that I fucked someone else and lied to you. You are a moron."

Gary had heard enough. He couldn't take any more pain that night. "I need some time to think," he said as he turned around, walked out of the trailer, started his car and drove away."

***

As Gary's relationship with Rachael seemed to be imploding, his best friend, Steve, was rekindling his relationship with an old flame.

Steve had never stopped loving Becky Jacobs. They had drifted apart after high school, but he always loved her, and Becky felt the same for him. She was pregnant with his baby but hadn't told him about it. It was tricky. She didn't want to hold him back or miss her chance to live her life — whatever that was.

But even though they really didn't want to be apart, had it not been for Dorothy Raymond, they may not have seen each other again. Both were young and stupid. Both were stubborn. Neither wanted to admit to the other that they needed each other. But Dorothy Raymond knew they belonged together, and she reasoned that all they needed was a little push.

So, she invited Becky to dinner to talk and catch up on things. Becky assumed dinner would only be with Dorothy and Earl Raymond. She really wasn't sure if she wanted to go but was curious about Steve and not ready to admit they had drifted as far apart as they had.

Dorothy called her son and invited him to dinner too, and he never suspected he'd see Becky. It was a Sunday evening dinner, after church, a family meal.

According to Dorothy, the dining room was uncomfortable when the two first sat down at the table. They weren't rude. They had said hi, and Becky explained that she was invited, but it was awkward. Earl, not known as a conversationalist, sat silent for a time, too. Prayer was given, then food was passed around in the quiet. Even the presence of Dorothy's famous double-fried chicken, homemade mashed potatoes and gravy, green bean casserole and buttermilk biscuits didn't seem to uncork the silence.

So, she talked. Dorothy had always had a gift for gab and decided to bombard her captive audience with small talk. They didn't know what was coming.

"Did you hear about old man Johnson from down the block? You know his wife died about three months ago, I guess, now. Cancer, from what I heard. She was such a young thing, too, fifty-five, I believe. People always figured that her husband would go first. He was a good ten years older than she was. He drank a lot, you know, and he smoked like a chimney. I had heard that his health wasn't very good. I always liked Myrtle. Well, about two weeks ago, Henry

Johnson remarried. He didn't even have a proper mourning period. The girl he married is a young thing, a good twenty, maybe thirty years younger than Henry. They say that they only dated for a couple of weeks before getting married. I think she married that old geezer for his money. Rumor has it that he had a large life insurance policy on Myrtle. Heck, people also say that even without that life insurance, Henry is worth a lot of money. He was the manager of the First National bank of Springfield for a decade before he retired, and he sure as heck didn't spend the money on Myrtle or the house or the broken-down car he drove. Anyway, he bought his new bride a brand new Cadillac. And, Gladys, my friend from across the block, said she saw his bride wearing what looked like a full-length mink coat when the two of them were going out to dinner a few nights ago.

"You wouldn't ever do that to me, would you, Earl?"

"Do what, Dorth?" he replied, lifting his head from the plate of food in front of him.

"Marry some young girl right after I died," she replied.

"No, hun. I think I'd wait at least a year to do that."

"Darn, Earl. It's not funny. Love is something that only comes around once in most people's lives. You got to cherish it while it lasts, and you've got to hold on to its memory long after it's gone."

"Don't you think so, Becky?"

"Ye-yes. Yes, of course."

Dorothy made an impression even though it was an obvious stunt. Things lightened up after that, and Steve was quick to apologize for his mother as soon as the meal was over. But the ice was broken. And there they were. Talking.

They began seeing each other again immediately. Their love for each other could not be denied, and they never were so foolish as to pretend it didn't matter as much as anything.

So, as Gary's love life was crashing and burning, Steve's was fresh with hope and starting to grow again.

***

Gary slept in his car the night of his argument with Rachael. He was pissed, but mainly he was hurt. He couldn't stop thinking about her, no matter how hard he tried. The next morning, he returned to the trailer and resolved to make up with Rachael. He wanted to tell her that he loved her and was willing to do whatever she wanted him to resolve the troubles they were in. He couldn't believe she might have meant the awful things she said. She was just scared. Even though he knew she must have cheated, he just could not accept she was so cold. He knew and fell in love with a different Rachael. He just had to get her back. Maybe she'd calmed down.

But when he got to the trailer, he found tables turned, couch cushions ripped apart, drawers opened, and their contents were thrown on the floor.

And Rachael was gone. Soon after, he filed a missing person report with the Nixa Police Department.

That evening he called his friend. Steve could hear the anguish in his voice. Steve cared about his friend and wanted to help. Getting back with Becky reminded him of what was important, so he met with Gary at a small neighborhood bar on Main Street near the Nixa town square. The place was called Dudley's. They had been in the bar only twice before. Dudley's was small and narrow, with a long oak wood bar about twenty feet long that spanned the entire length of one side. Against the other side of the wall was a single row of tables. The entire place, when packed, could only hold about thirty people.

Dudley's was nearly empty the night Steve and Gary met. Gary was waiting for him at the end of the bar when Steve walked in. He had been drinking for a while. His words were slow and slurred. Steve was glad the bar was busy so he could make out what his friend was saying.

"Buddy, you know that you're the only real friend I've got," Gary said once they sat down and got past the initial small talk. "Rachael has disappeared. We had a big fight. She cheated on me. She told me herself. Then she told me that she was never pregnant. She just told me she was and that I was the father to try to get money out of me.

"And now she's gone, Steve. I don't know if she ran away or if someone took her. I spent the night that we fought in my car, in a parking lot a couple of miles away. When I went back to the trailer the next morning, she was gone. But the trailer was a mess. Someone had ransacked it. It looked like a robbery."

"Did you report it to the police?" Steve was still unaware of the danger Gary was in. The pair were best friends, but Gary had never told his buddy about the plan to rob Harley or how everything had gone terribly wrong. Steve only knew there had been a fire at Rachael's, and she and the kids were staying with Gary for a time.

"Yes, this morning, I reported that Rachael was missing and that it looked like someone had robbed my mother's trailer."

"What did they say?"

"They asked if I knew of anything missing. I didn't. Hell, the place was a mess. Something might have been missing, but I didn't know for sure."

"Have they come by to investigate?"

"No, you know the Nixa cops. They have better things to do than investigate a small-time robbery that might not even be a robbery."

"Yeah, but it was more than that. You said that Rachael was missing. They would certainly investigate that."

"No, they said that she hadn't been gone long enough, and besides, they seem to think that since we had an argument the night before, that she may have messed up the trailer and then ran off."

"Shit, what about your mother? Is she OK? Did she see

or hear anything?"

"She's fine, and no, she didn't see or hear anything. Mom is on oxygen. The machine is pretty loud. Besides, she takes medication to help her sleep at night. She didn't hear a thing."

"Are the police going to do anything?"

"They took my information and said they would stop by the trailer and take a look when they had time. Right now, I'm just worried about Rachael. We had a terrible fight. I just hope she is OK."

Steve wanted to tell his friend that none of this about Rachael surprised him, that he knew what type of woman she was long before Gary figured it out. But he knew that wouldn't help matters. He wanted to be there for him, and his best friend was in pain. He wanted to just listen.

There was more on Gary's mind than a broken heart and concern for Rachael, of course. And Steve could sense it. Gary was nervous, shaking, and anxious. He could tell there was more bothering him.

"Gary, I can tell something else is going on, something you're holding back. You can tell me what it is. Maybe I can help."

Gary ordered another beer and a whiskey chaser. It downed a frosty mug of Bud in five gulps, then chugged the shot of whiskey. He needed a refill of liquid courage before he told his friend what he needed to say.

"I've got to tell you something. I can't hold it inside me anymore, and I have no one else that I can confide in. Remember the robbery at Grand Beach Park, the guy that got shot?"

"Yeah, I heard about it," Steve said.

"I was there. Rachael was there. We planned on robbing him."

"Oh, shit, Gary. Damn, I can't believe you would ever do anything like that."

"I thought Rachael was pregnant. She needed the money. The guy was a jerk. He was trying to get her in bed. That's what she told me. It was lies, but I didn't know it at the time. I just wanted to help. She was getting so distant, and she needed me. It was her idea. I know how stupid the plan was now, and I can't believe I bought into it. But the fact is, I did. I guess I was desperate to help her. I thought if I did, we could get married. It was stupid."

They paused for a minute. Steve was trying to look his friend in the eyes. Gary mostly kept his head down. Then, he continued.

"To make it even worse, I brought a gun. Rachael insisted on it. He was a big guy, a biker. She didn't think the robbery could work if I didn't show him a gun."

"Fuck, Gary. Are you the one that shot him?"

"No, Steve. I could never shoot someone. It was only for show. Hell, I didn't even have any bullets in it."

"Then who shot him and took his money?"

"I don't know. The robbery happened before I got there. I was just entering the park when I heard the gunshots, three of them. I was scared shitless. I hid behind some trees for a couple of minutes and then worked my way to where Rachael was. I was scared to death she'd been shot. When I got close. She ran to me. I could see the guy lying on the ground. Rachael had blood all over her. She told me two guys had robbed Harley, the guy she was with, the one we were going to rob. She was hysterical."

"So, did you see the two guys?"

"No. But a witness said they saw two guys in a white van speed off just after the gunshots, and I remember seeing a white van in a parking lot in the park when I got there."

"Wow. Holy cow, Gary. I don't know what to say. So, Rachael was with Harley, the biker. And she wanted you to rob Harley. Did this Harley guy know the guys who actually did it?"

"Well, Harley was sort of passed out when the robbery happened. He was real drunk and supposedly didn't know what was going on. He's said he doesn't know the two men that robbed and shot him. He thinks Rachael and I were involved."

"Why's that?" Steve asked.

"Well, he sort of found out that Rachael and I had been seeing each other. And remember the gun that I said I took with me? Well, I sort of dropped it in the park."

"Shit," Steve said. He was realizing the gravity of the situation. This was bad news. Gary was in over his head.

"The police already knew that Rachael was with Harley when he was shot. The cab driver that drove us home must have reported the blood stains that were all over Rachael. Well, when they found the gun and ran the serial number, it must have come back to my father. It didn't take very long for them to figure out I was in the park too."

"A day later, they brought me and Rachael in to talk. It came out that we were seeing each other. When Harley got out of his coma a week or so later, the police confronted him with questions about Rachael and me. He denied that a robbery took place. He denied that Rachael was there with him. In fact, he said he had no idea how he got to the park or why someone would shoot him. And Rachael had taken him there. He just acted like he didn't know anything. And the day after Harley got out of the hospital, someone burned down Rachael's house."

"Damn, I knew she was staying with you. I knew there had been a fire. Was it Harley? It had to be him, right? Gary, I'm worried. You need to go away somewhere, someplace that maniac won't find you."

"I think it's too late for that, buddy," Gary said, now fully realizing himself just how dangerous the situation was. "He knows where I live. He left Rachael a letter last night at the bar. He wants $40,000 by tomorrow night, or he's going to hurt us."

"What are you and Rachael going to do, Gary?"

"Rachael made it clear last night that she's not going to do anything. Maybe that's why she disappeared. I'd rather think that than think something terrible happened to her. She told me last night that she was leaving everything up to me."

"What?"

"Yeah, she thinks she has a pretty convincing story about what happened that night and thinks Harley will believe her. They had been fooling around for a while. Met at the bar. She was a liar, Steve. She was going behind my back. She thinks it'll be easy for him to believe I found out about their affair, became jealous, followed them to the park and robbed him, then took her home. She's running to him like it's all my fault. I wasn't even the one who shot him. I was only there for her."

Gary's eyes welled up with tears. Steve felt sick for his friend.

"So, what are you going to do?" Steve asked gently.

"The letter he left for her demanded that we drop the money off at a specific location tomorrow night at midnight. I was able to get my hands on sixty dollars. I figured I'd write a letter explaining everything that happened that night and ask him to accept all I got to give and then leave it all for him, hoping he believes me. I don't know what else to do. I didn't rob the guy. But I'm afraid he'll just come after me."

"Oh, Gary. I don't know. I'm not sure that's going to work," Steve said.

"Well, I've got to try something, and that's the best idea I can come up with."

Gary thought a little more about what his friend had said. "Maybe I could add to the note that I want to make things right, and I could pay a little at a time, like on installments."

"Yeah, at least that would show you're willing to make things right," Steve said, unsure of what else to say. It was a bad spot.

"Buddy, I know I don't have a right to ask you," Gary asked in a desperate-sounding voice, "but could you please come with me tomorrow night to make the drop-off? I'm afraid he might be there, waiting for me. If I have someone with me, he is less likely to do anything, if you know what I mean. You don't even need to get out of the car. Leave it running. I'll get out, make the drop and get back in the car. The whole thing shouldn't take more than a couple of minutes, and we will be on our way back."

"Damn, I don't know, Gary. If that guy burned down Rachael's house. He sounds like a maniac."

"Well, I hope he might be more pissed at Rachael than he is at me. Especially if he reads my letter. He doesn't know me. He just knows what she said. And he did burn her house down. But Rachael said he's serious, and if she's telling him lies and then he's out there hiding in the woods waiting for money, and I don't come, then I think he might really be after me, you know. This might be my only way to tell him my side."

"Oh, Gary. I need another beer," Steve said. They sat for several minutes in silence. Steve wanted to help his friend but had a bad feeling about this.

Steve knew somehow in his gut if Gary did this alone, he wouldn't come back from those woods. His mind was made up. He sighed deeply, then motioned for Gary to look him in the eye.

"I'll stay in the car."

CHAPTER 10
THE OUTSIDERS

"Rose honey, can you bring us a couple of pieces of that blueberry pie? My friend is looking a little hungry."

"I thought you said it turned your shit a weird color," she responded.

"Yeah, but those don-nuts you served us seemed to have completely stopped me up. I figure that blueberry pie of yours might be enough to unclog me, sort of like drano works on a clogged sink. It may not look pretty coming out, but it sure beats being stuck inside."

"Damn, you do have a gift for words, Booger. You should write Hallmark cards," Rose replied with a sarcastic tone. "You want your pie warmed with a scoop of ice cream?"

"Yes, but this time warm the pie before you put the ice

cream on top."

A couple of minutes later, Rose returned to the table with two pieces of pie, ice cream on top and a pot of coffee.

"If I were you, Booger, I'd wait a few minutes to eat that pie. Norm's about to clean that bathroom, and if you use it before he gets in there, I'm afraid the stench might be enough to kill him."

"Yeah, well, there are probably worse ways to die," he responded.

"I sincerely doubt that," Rose said with a grin.

After Rose left the table, I asked Booger what I'd wanted to know ever since I had met him.

"So, what exactly happened to Steve and Gary?" I asked.

Booger took another bite of his pie, then a sip of coffee, then he sat back in the booth and took a long drag on his cigar. It was a thick cigar. He had been smoking it for over an hour. It was down to the last few drags. I wasn't sure if he heard what I had asked or if maybe he was just thinking about my question, considering what to say.

"No one knows for sure what happened. We know that Steve drove Gary down to a desolate place in the Ozarks off route 110. At least, that is what he told his girlfriend, Becky, before he left. She begged him not to go. We also know that his car was found about a week later, down an embankment, overturned and burned. Neither boy was found. After that, everything that happened to those boys is purely speculation.

"I drove down to see the spot where the car was found. The road was narrow with sharp turns. It happened on a stretch of road winding down one side of a mountain deep in the Ozarks. Seeing that the boys went down there around midnight, the road had to be treacherous in the dark, particularly for someone that was not used to driving it. It was certainly believable that Steve simply lost control of the car, and it rolled down the mountain and caught fire. That's what the police thought that investigated the accident."

"What did you think, Booger?"

"I thought it was odd that no bodies were found. I thought it was odd that no blood was found in the car or that the package Gary brought with the money and note in it wasn't found in the car or anywhere around the area. I especially found it curious that there was zero evidence that the boys were even in that car. There were no skid marks left on the road, no indication of how the car lost control but more than anything else, the boys were never found. Even after searching the backwoods around the accident sight, there was no evidence that the boys had left the scene of the accident."

"So, what did the police do?"

"Nothing, as far as I could tell. After a few hours of looking for anyone that might have been in the car, the local police gave up looking any further. Hell, the police weren't even certain that anyone was in the car. They speculated that someone might have pushed the car off the road and down the mountain. It appeared to be an old, beat-up car. Perhaps it had outlived its usefulness."

"What about the license plate on the car. Didn't they look that up and determine that Steve Raymond was the owner, then contact his family."

"Well, that was another weird thing about the accident. The license plate on the car was missing, and the VIN # on the dashboard was completely destroyed in the fire. They had no idea of knowing who owned that car. It was towed away a day later and destroyed at a salvage yard. I did go down to Branson to talk to the sheriff who investigated the accident. It was nearly nine months after it happened," Booger said, taking another bite of the pie.

"How did that go?" I asked.

"About how I expected it to. He told me that I was fishing without any bait. He had investigated a hundred other accidents on Ozark roads. Mainly outsiders drinking, smoking weed and driving too fast. That this accident appeared no different than the others, except there were no bodies to scrape off the road.

"I asked him why no blood was found, why no bodies were recovered?

"He said that maybe it wasn't an accident after all. Maybe someone just wanted to get rid of the car by pushing it off the road and down the side of that mountain.

"'And they removed the license plate before they did it?'" I asked the sheriff.

"That's when he got pissed. That's when he said something that I'll never forget."

"I know why you're here. You're investigating the drownings of those two boys at S of O. Well, let me tell you something, city boy with your fancy, red sports car and your $100 cowboy boots and hat, as far as I'm concerned, those boys were drunk and taking drugs when they got in that water and drown. And, even if something different happened to them, I'm certain they got what was coming to them. People in these parts don't take kindly to outsiders coming in and causing trouble. And right now, Mr. Booger McLain, I think you're an outsider coming in trying to cause trouble. It's best for you to go back from where you came and stop sticking your nose in other people's business.' The strange thing was, son, that I never mentioned those two boys that drowned. There had never been any connection made between the car accident and those two boys. That sheriff appeared to know a lot more than he eluded to."

"So, what did you do next?"

"I left town. A Branson police car provided me an escort until I got outside the city limits."

"Ok, but you must have an opinion about what happened to the boys on the trip to make the drop-off?"

"Well, I know that if it looks like a turd, smells like a

turd, and you find yourself wiping your ass afterward, then there's a pretty good chance you've just dropped a turd. What I think doesn't mean a damn thing. It's what I can prove, and I can't prove diddly squat.

"We know they left to make the drop off that night. That's what Becky told the Raymonds anyway, and that's what the Raymonds told the police when they filed a missing person's report on their son.

"We assume the car that was found at the bottom of the mountain was Steve's. Becky was at Steve's apartment when the two of them left in Steve's car, and the police description of the car found at the bottom of the mountain was very similar to the one Steve drove. Then there was what happened immediately after the boys disappeared."

"What was that, Booger?"

"Damn it, Rose. What does a man have to do to get another cup of coffee around here?"

"Keep your pants on, old man."

"Damn, I would have thought the opposite, Rose. I figured you'd want me to take my pants off to get your attention."

"Dream on, Booger. Hell, at your age, I'd probably give you a heart attack if I did give in to you."

"Yeah, well, if a man's got to go, I can't think of a better way."

Then Booger lit up a fresh stogie, took a few puffs and

turned his attention to me.

"So, what did you ask, son?"

"You were about to tell me what happened after the two boys disappeared."

"Oh yeah, well, there were a series of odd events, misfortunes, I guess you'd say," he began. "First was when Harley was seen going into Billy Bobs. He was looking for Rachael. We know that he talked to the night bartender who worked the same shift she did. And we know that he talked to the manager. They both told the police that he was agitated and threatening. He wanted to know where she was staying and if they had spoken to her. They both denied hearing from her or knowing where she was staying. He asked if the bar owed her any money and if she was expecting a paycheck. That's when the manager and the bartender's story didn't exactly follow the same path. The manager said that she wasn't owed any money and so she wasn't expecting a paycheck. The bartender said that the employees were paid only once a month and that he was certain she hadn't been paid for the last week or so that she had worked."

"From what I knew of Harley, I don't think he would have handled being lied to very well. But that is only speculation, mind you. Anyway, the bar burned down a couple of nights later, after closing time. No one was around, and no one was injured in the fire. Like I said, it was an odd event, a misfortune.

"The cause of the fire was never determined. One arson investigator found the fire suspicious and could have been caused by an accelerant based on the source of the fire being so close to the back door. But a second arson investigator noted that the fire appeared to have started near an electrical outlet in a storage area with flammable supplies nearby. He felt that the fire could have been accidental.

"Both the bartender and the manager told the police about their strange encounter with Harley, but without definitive proof that the fire was the result of arson, no further investigation was done."

"So, if Harley burned down Billy Bobs, do you think it was just because the manager had lied to him?"

"Son, no one is saying that Harley had anything to do with that fire. Don't put words in my mouth. Like I said, the police never determined how the fire began.

"We do know that the manager of the bar, a man by the name of Tony, filed a police report a few days later. He reported employee files missing from a fireproof cabinet in his office. He also reported that money was missing from the safe in his office. He thought it was about $500."

"Did the police investigate?"

"No. They chalked his report of a crime up to a vain attempt to get the insurance company to pay off his claim. You see, Tony was having a lot of trouble getting the insurance company to release the money. Without a determination about how the fire was started, the insurance company was stalling payment of his claim. If the police had determined that the fire may have been the result of covering up a robbery, he would have likely got the insurance proceeds he needed."

Booger was a difficult man to figure. He talked, he talked a lot, but he refused to speculate about anything. He only talked about facts, about absolutes. He may have liked me, OK. He may have accepted me. But he sure as hell didn't trust me enough to tell me what he was thinking. Still, I had to ask him again.

"What do you think happened to Billy Bobs?"

"I think a fire of unknown origins burned the place down." Then he continued. "But I must admit that what happened afterward left me scratching my head.

"Two days later, a detective from the Springfield police department, along with the Nixa sheriff, paid a visit to Gary's mother's trailer. The detective was following up on the missing person's report filed by the Raymond family. The sheriff came along with the detective because the trailer was in Nixa, MO, an area out of Springfield's jurisdiction. The detective had a few questions for Mrs. Walker. He had no idea that Rachael was living there, too. The Raymonds had reported, and Becky confirmed that Steve was last seen leaving his apartment with Gary Walker. The detective was hopeful that Mrs. Walker may have heard from her son or perhaps had an idea where he might be.

"What they found in that trailer was a shock. A woman's body, presumed to be in her thirties or forties, was lying face down on a sofa in the living room. Next to her on a coffee table was what looked like crystal meth. In the bedroom, they discovered Mrs. Walker with an empty oxygen tank near her bedside and a breathing tube unattached. She had been dead for at least two days, the coroner estimated. Both bodies were in the beginning state of decomposition. A few days later, they identified the body on the sofa as Rachael. The presumed cause of death was an overdose. A large quantity of meth was found in her system.

"Rachael's death would be ruled an accident. It was determined that she had taken a lethal dose of drugs. Mrs. Walker's death was ruled a result of natural causes. She was an elderly, sickly woman dependent on an oxygen supply to breathe normally. She was bedridden and dependent on others for her care. It was thought that when the oxygen supply ran out, she was unable to breathe properly on her own and simply passed away.

"The Raymonds refused to believe that story. They were certain something more sinister had happened to them. They were certain the deaths of Rachael and Gary's mother were connected to the disappearance of their son. But they had no evidence. The police refused to investigate further."

"Why, Booger?" There were so many connections to those two boys' disappearances and to Harley. Why didn't they investigate Harley?"

"Son, you've got a lot to learn about the Ozarks. The entirety of this area, from Springfield south to the Arkansas border and east to the Oklahoma line, is full of contrasts everywhere you look and in nearly every person you see.

"The Ozarks is a resort area, a place where city people come to retire or bring their families for vacation. It's a place dependent on an image that is completely in contrast to reality. Guarding that image is a necessity to preserving the livelihood of the people that live here year around.

"I suspect that most hill people, hell, most lifelong residents of this area, hate the tourists, hate outsiders of any type. They don't trust them, and they don't want them here. The flavor of the Ozarks changes drastically once you get south of the bedroom communities surrounding Springfield. The contrasts in people and attitudes are about as different as night and day. To the hill people of the Ozarks, Springfield is not a part of the Ozarks. They are suspicious of its people as much as they are any outsider. You see, they believe that Springfield has been swallowed up by city folks that have moved down here to start a new life. They believe that Springfield has sold its soul and is populated by people who only want to use the Ozarks for their own personal gain. They have seen progress swallow up the Ozarks one acre at a time. They blame city people for that, and to a large degree, they blame Springfield.

"Harley was one of them, a hill person, a good old boy and as such, he was insulated by people that didn't trust outsiders.

"You ask why the Springfield police didn't investigate Harley? It was because they were afraid. You just don't jump into a pit of rattlesnakes without expecting to get bit.

"The Ozarks is a majestic place. The beauty of the lakes in the valley, with the warm morning sun glistening off of their surface and illuminating the tall oak trees surrounding it, is something most people will never forget. But every morning is followed by nightfall, and that's when the dark underbelly of the Ozarks comes out to play.

"I saw that darkness one night, and that was the last time I went to the Ozarks."

"What happened?"

"No, I haven't got to that point yet. There's still a lot of the story you haven't heard yet," Booger replied. Booger took another sip of coffee. "Damn, it's cold. Rose, be a darling and bring some more coffee."

The evening rush had begun. I looked around, and all the tables were filled. So were the chairs at the counter. A second waitress and one more cook had joined Rose behind the counter. We had been sitting at the same spot for nearly ten hours. My ass ached. My bladder felt like it was swimming in a sea of coffee. I had never drunk that much coffee in my life and had never seen anyone drink that much coffee. I was excusing myself to go to the bathroom about every thirty minutes now. And, I was amazed that I had seldom seen Booger go over that time, three times to my count. Where he was holding it was a mystery that I would never solve. I speculated that he was wearing a diaper under those jeans, something very absorbent, something that could hold a lot of pee.

Before Rose returned to the table with refills, Booger excused himself and went to the restroom for a fourth time that day. I watched him go, looking for any diaper lines or possibly the signs of an accidental leak as he went. There weren't any.

Rose appeared with a pot of coffee a few seconds later. She took a seat across from me. "Hope you don't mind," she said. I've been on my feet all day. I get off in another hour, but my legs and feet have already reached closing time."

"No, I don't mind," I said. "If you don't mind me asking, how long have you known Booger?"

"Ever since I started working here, about ten years, I guess. You know Booger's not his real name. It's Horace," she said in a whisper. "Don't tell him that I told you. Horace was his father's name. He was the oldest son, named after his dad. His daddy went to prison. He murdered someone, fist fight in a bar, I heard. Ever since then, he went by the name of Booger. Said it was a nickname his friends gave him because he had the longest, nastiest boogers any of them had ever seen. Booger told me that, but I don't believe the story. The man bullshits more than anyone that I've ever known. But you know what?"

"What?" I asked.

"Don't you dare ever tell him this, but down deep inside, no better, more honest, more caring man ever existed. I could tell you stories about him that you just wouldn't believe. But it's safe to say that even though on the outside he appears rough and unforgiving, inside he is a teddy bear."

I wanted to hear what Rose had to say about Booger, but our conversation was cut short. Booger came out of the restroom and directly to the table.

"What are you two talking about?" he asked.

"I was just asking your friend if I needed to clean up some of the manure you were trying to feed him," Rose responded.

"Well, contrary to your belief, Rose. Most people like my brand of manure."

"Sure, they do, old man," she said as she walked away from the table.

"Tell me, Booger. Was it soon after the bodies of Rachael and Gary's mom were found in that trailer that the bodies of those two boys were discovered floating in Lake Honor?"

"No, not really. I believe it was about four more weeks before their bodies were discovered. But that doesn't mean that they weren't already dead. From what I understood in my investigation, the coroner ruled their deaths to be caused by accidental drowning almost immediately after they were discovered. There was no autopsy, no attempt to narrow the window of when that drowning might have occurred.

"Hell, they were in too big of a rush to rule the deaths an accident to care when or how it might have happened."

"From what I understood, S of O has plenty of friends, some very powerful. Most wanted the news of those deaths to go away as quickly as possible. The school didn't want or need that kind of bad publicity."

"The only evidence we have of a timeline of their deaths was what happened to Becky Jacobs about a week after the bodies were discovered in the trailer."

CHAPTER 11
A FRESH START

Becky Jacobs was not born and raised in Springfield. Her parents moved there when she was twelve years old. She was not happy about it. She had grown up in a quiet suburb on the southwest side of St. Louis, a place called Crestwood. They lived in a modest home. Her father worked at Monsanto. Her mother was a stay-at-home mom. A downturn in the economy in the mid-sixties resulted in the layoff of her father. The move to Springfield would be a fresh start. The 3M plant was hiring, and although they paid considerably less than Monsanto, the cost of living in Springfield was lower, offsetting the wage difference.

Becky had a lot of friends in Crestwood. She was charming, outgoing and smart. Crestwood was a growing suburb back then, full of young families with children. She enjoyed her life there and didn't want to leave it behind. The move, happening when it did, gave an edge to her teenage years no one would have suspected before. She would find plenty of friends and adjust, but always feel like the city kid who had no say in the decision to move.

It was an uncomfortable transition for Becky. The city of a hundred thousand people was growing, but still a fraction of the roughly two million people in Greater St. Louis. The "Queen City of the Ozarks" was a stop on America's highway, Route 66—conveniently about halfway between well-established regional hubs of St. Louis and Tulsa, Okla. It had a handful of movie theatres, an abundance of fast food restaurants, gas stations and motels that littered the stretch of Chestnut Expressway, which ran east to west as part of the historic highway's original business loop, and Business 65, aka Glenstone Ave., which ran north to south. It was a place for people to fill up their tanks, get a bite to eat or maybe spend the night before continuing on to somewhere else— camping, the lakes, south to Arkansas, west to California. It had its share of blue-collar manufacturing jobs, a couple of colleges, plenty of single-family homes, low crime, and an abundance of churches and decent schools—but for a twelve-year-old, it felt a world away from the diverse, bustling home she knew.

Springfield of the late 60s was something between a

backdrop of American Graffiti and Norman Rockwell. It was conservative, white and limited. Teenagers and young adults cruised Kearney Street on the north side at night, waving down friends and meeting new ones. Its new flagship southside shopping center, The Battlefield Mall, opened in 1970. The "battlefield" it referred to was the Battle of Wilson's Creek, the first major Civil War battle west of the Mississippi, which took place southwest of town and reflected its soul as a place between. A place in the middle. Not South or North, East or West. It was both ever-changing and never changing. It was both too big to have the quaint charm of a small town and too small to have the modernity of a metropolis. It was a place where the winds changed quickly — a wholesome city on a plateau, both below the tops of the nearby rolling hills and above valleys and dense backwoods. It was both a rest stop and a place to lay down roots.

Much like the weather in southwest Missouri, everything was changing quickly for Becky. Being uprooted from her home coincided with puberty, new social pressures, and new everything. She felt like a stranger in her own life. She was socially adept but often withdrew to the library, her bedroom, or any quiet spaces she could find. She was outwardly holding it all together but always seeking peace, balance, and belonging. She made friends but was in no one's inner circle. She blamed her father. She blamed the move. She always felt like an outsider.

With time, memories of her youth in the St. Louis suburb would fade and be replaced with new friendships and new memories. She would grow to love Springfield and the people who called it their home. It was a good town, wholesome and safe, and there was value in that.

But beneath the surface, nothing was pure. Like any city, alcohol, drugs and prostitution were the dirty little secrets that complicated the perfect Route 66 stop.

Al's drive-in, off of Business 65, was where she first met Steve Raymond. She was a freshman in high school. Al's was her first job. She was fifteen, working as a car hop. Al's was a hot spot for teenagers to grab a bite to eat, a cold, thick malt or just mingle with their friends. It was a drive-in reminiscent of the Sonic drive-in that populated suburbs and smaller towns today. There were only a handful of tables inside, but outside, there were rows of picnic tables under a large canopy, and there were double rows of parking spots with menu boards. Car hops serviced the cars parked in rows along both sides of the drive-in and the customers seated at the picnic tables outside.

Becky had taken the job three months earlier at the beginning of the summer, the drive-in's busiest season. Her goal was to earn enough money to buy a car when she turned sixteen in four more months.

The restaurant seemed to always be in need of help. Work was hard, and the pay was low. Employees would come and go. Frank, the owner of Al's drive-in, wasn't the easiest person to work for. A retired sergeant in the Marine Corp., he bought Al's soon after he retired after twenty years of service. Frank was still young, entering the Marine Corps when he was a teenager. He was on the backstretch of thirty now. The Marines had taught him a disciplined, regimented lifestyle that would dominate his management style and would not sit well with the coming-of-age teenagers that were his workforce.

He was, from all accounts, a good man, fair and honest, but he was not a person that compromised. Late to work, you were fired. Not do what you were told, fired. Call in sick too often, fired. Talk back to him or argue, fired.

Frank was constantly hiring and training new workers. That was what brought Steve into Al's drive-in that day. He had been working construction that summer, small jobs, mainly clean-up and running errands. But the construction season was slowing down. It was the last few days of summer. He needed a part-time job that he could work through the school year.

"Do you have any experience as a fry cook?" Frank asked.

"No," Steve responded.

"Have you ever worked in a restaurant before?"

"No," he responded again.

"Do you have a girlfriend or play sports or take piano

lessons or do any activities that will interfere with work?"

"No."

"Are you a religious person, someone that gets offended easily by cuss words?"

"No."

"Do your parents need you home at a specific time?"

"No."

"Are you concerned about hard work, long hours and low pay?"

"No."

"Then, son, let me ask you. What the hell is wrong with you?

"Frank put Steve to work that day. The entirety of his training lasted about twenty minutes. Frank didn't have the patience or the time to babysit anyone. He put people's natural survival instincts to the test from the very beginning.

"'You either learn to swim, or you drown,' was one of his favorite sayings. There was no room for people that couldn't or wouldn't take their own initiative. The strongest, most creative and most disciplined leaders were the ones that would survive any prolonged period of time working at Al's. There were very few of those people. Steve was one. Becky was another.

"It was only a matter of time before they would fall in love. Although, in the beginning, it wasn't exactly love at first sight. Steve was quiet, reserved, and seemed distant to most of the other workers at Al's. Becky was more outgoing and popular, even with her quiet edge. She was also quite attractive. Steve noticed that the first time he saw her picking up a customer's order off the preparation counter directly in front of his grill. "She was so beautiful," he would tell his friends later, recounting how they first met. "She was easily the most beautiful girl that I'd ever met. But she didn't exactly feel the same attraction to me. To her, I was just another fry cook, just another boy.

"Becky was in no hurry to date. "Boys are so juvenile, so transparent, so single-minded," she once told a friend. That's how she felt about Steve at first. She was picking up an order for a customer, checking it over for accuracy. "Damn," she said, looking down at the hamburger in front of her. "Hey, fryboy," she yelled, looking directly at Steve. The ticket said no onions. I even underlined the 'no.' And, surprise, this burger is loaded with onions." Steve, stood there looking at her, mouth open, frozen in place and unable to speak back. She was so attractive. He didn't know what to say. Becky waited, but he just stood there. She put the plate down and said, "Just remake it," she said as she mumbled under her breath, "boys are useless."

"Two days later, both were working the same shift when Becky came back to prep an order for one of her customers. Next to the serving tray of burgers and fries was a single Prairie Aster flower, referred to as a sunflower by

local folk because it resembles a sun on a warm summer day
with a bright yellow bud in the center surrounded by white or
purple petals jetting out like rays of sunlight. Steve had heard
her telling one of her friends the day before that it was her
favorite flower, and she hadn't known he was around.

"The flower was the first of many left with no note. He
would leave her one every day she worked while they were
in season. It was even left on days that Steve wasn't working.
It might be left at the beginning of her shift or sometime in
the middle, or perhaps at the very end of her shift. She never
saw him leave it, so it took a long time before she realized it
was him. He never told her that he was the one leaving it. It
became a highlight of her day. No matter how difficult her day
was, that flower changed everything. When Fall arrived, the
flowers stopped. But, when the Spring began again, and the
wildflowers began to bloom, the daily flower would reappear
on her counter.

"By the time he was saying "hi" to her all the time at
school and angling for dinner with her parents, she figured
he was the one. Curiously, they never talked about how the
flower appeared the days and nights she worked at Al's.
By the time they were dating, she knew that Steve was the
flower guy. She had ruled everyone else out. And he knew
that Becky knew he left it. But it remained unsaid. It was their
little secret. The reminder of a love no one else knew about.

"Becky put that first flower in her diary as a keepsake. In

time, it faded, wilted and turned crisp and fragile, eventually falling apart. But its memories never left her.

"Becky and Steve never dated anyone else. Neither wanted to. Disagreements were rare. Arguments were even more rare. Their love was consummated on a late summer evening after their senior year, just before Becky started college and Steve started trade school. They had planned to wait, to seal their love on their wedding night, sometime in the future. Both were virgins. Both were hopeless romantics.

"But things were changing late that summer. For the first time since they met, both were heading in different directions. They had separate dreams and aspirations for their lives. They loved each other. They wanted to spend their lives together, but other desires were pulling them apart.

"After their time apart and reconnecting, they let go of their inhibitions one night under the stars, beneath the tall oak trees that garnished the hillside overlooking a small lake on the south side of town. They gave in to what they had both wanted so badly.

"There was a sort of guilt that both felt, lying in the grass after, holding each other tight. Neither was sorry for what had happened. They had both wanted it for so long, but they decided then and there that they'd wait until they got married before they'd do it again. Neither could know that day would never come.

"Within weeks, Becky would be battling nausea and

vomiting. She knew instinctively she was pregnant even before she took a pregnancy test. A trip to a local free medical clinic confirmed her suspicions. She didn't tell anyone, not her mother, not her friends and certainly not Steve. Besides, she wasn't showing yet.

"It gave her time to think, to decide what she wanted to do. She had dreams for her future. She wanted to become a nurse, maybe even a doctor. A baby would sidetrack, maybe even end, her career aspirations. And, then, there was Steve. If he knew about the baby, he would want to marry her. That was just how he was, grounded and responsible. Would she be forcing him into a life he didn't want? She was young and confused. Becky didn't know just what to do.

"She thought about giving birth. Maybe, giving up the baby and allowing a good family to adopt her child. But she knew that if she gave birth to the baby, it would be impossible to give it up.

"So, she thought about abortion. She even called a clinic in St. Louis that provided them. She got the information and even scheduled an appointment. Two days before that appointment, something happened that changed her mind. She went into the clinic, the same one that had confirmed she was pregnant. She needed to hear the heartbeat. She needed to say goodbye.

"The doctor obliged her request. He pulled out his stethoscope and found the rhythm. Bum-bum. Bum-bum.

Then, something unexpected happened. Her eyes filled with tears. That was the day that she fell in love all over again. That was the day that she knew that she could never go through with an abortion. That night, she drew a picture of her daughter — she knew somehow it would be a daughter — and labeled it "Emma." Looking at her completed drawing, she vowed to always love and protect her. They could be a family. Becky had been overthinking things. They could be a family. Steve would be happy, and she and her daughter could make him happy. They could have a fresh start.

CHAPTER 12
VEERING OFF ROAD

The dinner crowd had left, and only a handful of customers remained. Rose's shift was nearly over. She was removing dishes, cleaning tables, preparing to leave for the evening, and looking forward to a hot, soaking bath to soften the pain of her aching back and feet. This was the part of the day she looked forward to. Waitressing was hard work. It was hell on her feet, legs and back. Customers were rude, and tips were not a lot.

Ever since her divorce five years earlier, she had been alone. The loneliness bothered her at first. She's used to it now. More than used to it, she enjoyed it and craved time by herself after a long day's work. Life was hectic at the diner. She was always taking care of other people's needs. But at night, after work, in the quiet of her small, one-bedroom apartment, she could decompress and refuel.

Her ex-husband was a regional truck driver for a quarry near Sarcoxie. He rarely spent a night away from home. Looking back on it, she wished he had. Too much time together at home had been a problem.

She wanted kids. He didn't. She had a romantic view of marriage. He was much more traditional and selfish; he wanted a wife to cook, clean and take care of his needs. He also drank too much. He was abusive, emotionally and physically. Though she believed in the love of their courtship, it wasn't long before she was trapped in a loveless marriage. The drinking and abuse just got worse with time.

Despite his desire not to have children, he did get Rose pregnant once. He was not happy about it. When she was five months along, he beat the crap out of her one night for "disrespecting him in his home." She had refused to bring him a beer because he was obviously drunk. He knocked out two of her teeth, broke two ribs, and she lost her baby that night.

Rose called the police, and they took her husband away. Ten minutes after they hauled him off, she packed her bags and left. Without a dime to her name, she found her way to a women's shelter in Springfield. She lived there for the next year while her divorce was finalized.

Three weeks before she left the shelter, her ex-husband

was killed in a barfight. He had a knife. The other guy had a bigger knife. She didn't go to his funeral.

Rose started working at Joe's Diner a month before she moved out of the shelter. She had no experience as a waitress. Unless you count diffusing bullies or knowing how to cover up bruises with very little makeup.

At her interview, she discovered that Joe was not Joe. His actual name was Norman Joseph, Norm, they called him. The Joe in the diner's name was his father. His dad had started the restaurant thirty years earlier. He had inherited the business from his dad, who passed away from a heart attack only a few months earlier. The staff loved his father, and they had trouble accepting that a son, who was never very close to his father, who had gone to college and had a good job, would want or be capable of running a run-down hole-in-the-wall diner.

One by one, the staff found other jobs and left. The place was in need of repairs, outdated, and depressing. But Norm was determined to make it work. To prove those who had doubted him wrong. To carry on his father's legacy. It was the least he could do for the man that raised him after his mother died thirteen years earlier of cancer. His father worked long hours, seven days a week, to pay the bills and eventually to send his only child to college.

It was a good situation for Rose. He was desperate for help, and she was desperate for work. But there was more than a mutual need for each other's help. They connected immediately. They saw past the surface of each other. They recognized each other's loneliness and need for a home. And so, Joe's became her home.

"Rose, darling, can you fill up our coffee before you take off for your wild date?" Booger said with the charm of a snake oil salesman.

"The only wild date I've got tonight is with a hot, steamy bubble bath and a cold beer," she responded.

"A woman after my own heart," he replied. "Rose, you and I need to get together sometime, go dancing, hit the bars, maybe finish at my place for a little Perry Como and a night of untamed passion."

"Anytime, old man, anytime," she said with a wink and a smile.

Then she turned to me. "You know he says the same thing to me every night he's in here. If I ever took him up on his offer, I'd probably give the old geezer a heart attack."

As she turned to walk away, I could see Booger's hand reach out and drop a twenty-dollar bill in her pocket. "You be safe tonight, Rose. I want to see your smiling face tomorrow when I come in for the meatloaf special."

She didn't say anything, but I saw her smile.

"Booger, tell me what happened to Rachael and Becky after Steve and Gary left to make the money drop?"

"Well, son. That is a mystery that we will probably

never know. We only have a few pieces of facts to put together that puzzle.

"We know Steve and Gary left to take $60 and Gary's note to Harley explaining what happened down to the drop-off, according to Becky. We also know from the police reports Becky was with Steve just before he left and had made a last-minute plea for him not to go. She said, according to the report, she watched the two of them drive off. Supposedly, the need for the trip to take Harley money was expressed in a letter he gave Rachael.

"We also know the boys never came back from that trip. It seems the car they took ended up burnt to a crisp down a steep embankment, but not even that is certain. What happened to them on the way down or while they were making the drop, or on the way home? Nobody knows.

"Becky reported both Steve and Gary missing the next day. She told the police about their trip, the money Harley was demanding, the drop-off and the note and sixty dollars Gary took with him to leave at the drop sight. But she had no proof. The boys had taken the letter with the instructions so they could locate the drop-off location. It was late at night. They were going into the middle of nowhere.

"Becky was only able to provide a general idea of where the boys were going, off Highway 110 about ten miles northwest of Branson. Hell, it was the middle of the fucking Ozarks. There weren't street signs or maps that would pinpoint the location. The police even speculated that it was unlikely the boys ever found the drop-off.

"Becky did, however, give the police two bits of information that were helpful," Booger continued. "First, she told them that the letter was written by Harley. They had known that name from the shooting in the park a few weeks earlier. Harley was the victim. Second, Becky told them Harley left the letter for Rachael, that Rachael had read it and that she might know where the drop off was or perhaps even know where to find Harley."

"But they hadn't talked to Rachael, right?" I asked, appreciating the recap even if it meant extending the conversation further.

"No, they tried too. Becky told them she'd been staying in Gary's mother's trailer. She gave them the address. A little checking with the Nixa police showed that Gary had filed a police report of a possible burglary at that residence. He also reported Rachael missing. But no one had followed up."

"So, did they go to the trailer?"

"No, not right away. You see, there were some complications. Gary lived in Nixa. His mother's trailer was in Nixa. But Becky had filed the police report with the Springfield police. There was nothing they could do without the cooperation of the Nixa police department, and they weren't in a very cooperative mood. The Springfield police, it seemed, one month earlier had crossed jurisdictions in an effort to apprehend a robbery suspect that had committed the crime in Springfield and then led police on a high-speed chase across the Nixa city limits. A pedestrian was hit and killed, an elderly Nixa resident, during the chase.

"Regardless, the Springfield police had an opportunity to talk to Rachael. They just didn't realize it until it was too late. The girl was sitting in the County jail just five miles down the road from where Becky filed the police report. Talk about the left hand not knowing what the right hand was doing.

"She was arrested along with two older men leaving a party on a rural patch of land just west of Springfield. A group of young people had met there to party—booze and marijuana, mainly. It was the type of party that happens on a regular basis in the Ozarks. But this one turned ugly—a fight, knives were pulled, and a gun was fired. The police arrived just about the time a blue van raced away, nearly side-swiping a state trooper. The van didn't make it very far. Other police cars coming on the scene blocked the van's exit.

"Rachael and two guys were in the van. All three were wasted. A revolver was found, recently fired, underneath a passenger seat. Two ounces of blue crystal meth were also found in a small, plastic bag hidden in the glove compartment."

"They were arrested and taken to the County jail. This is when things get interesting. Two ounces of meth is a lot of drugs, enough certainly to warrant a felony charge. Then on top of it was firing a gun, one that, by the way, no one had a permit for and that just so happens didn't have a serial number. Add to that resisting arrest and what would later be determined, fleeing the scene in a stolen van. At least the van had no title and no registration, and the license plate, it turned out, had been lifted from someone else's car.

"The two men had no identification on them and, as it turned out, gave false names.

"They should have had the book thrown at them. They should have been locked up for some time, or at least the two men. The police really didn't have anything on Rachael. Yes, she was with them. Yes, she was intoxicated. But she wasn't driving. She didn't fire the gun. She didn't resist arrest. The only thing she was definitely guilty of was being a poor judge of character, particularly in the men she chose to hang out with.

"Anyway, the really interesting part is that the trio went in front of a judge the very next day. An attorney from Kansas City came down to bail them out and plead their case in front of a judge less than eight hours after they were arrested. The charges wound up being dropped, and all three were gone before the police were even aware they had given false names and false addresses. A run of the van's license plate came back to an elderly couple in Branson. That car had sat idle in their garage for nearly a year. They had no idea their license plate had been stolen."

"Shit, Booger," I replied, a little shell shocked from

what he had just said. "those two guys, in the van, with the gun, with Rachael, could they have been the two men that robbed and shot Harley that night in the park?"

"Hey, wait a second, son. Don't assume something that you can't prove. No one knows the identity of those two men that were at the party with Rachael, except maybe Rachael. And she sure as hell isn't talking about it."

"What about the van? What about the gun? What about the meth they found in the van?"

"Hey, remember, the van the three of them were in was blue color, a dark blue as I recall. The van seen pulling out of the park the night Harley was shot was white, according to witnesses."

"They could have painted it, Booger," I argued.

"Yes, they could have, but that is just speculation. There is no proof that they painted it. If you're going to be a real reporter someday, you have to stick with the facts, son.

"As for the gun and the meth they found, both disappeared from the evidence room not long after the three of them were released."

"Don't you find that suspicious?" I asked, trying to get any acknowledgement from Booger that some sort of conspiracy had taken place."

He seemed to think for a minute before answering, taking another sip of coffee, which was surely cold by this time and sitting back in his seat to take another drag from his cigar. Finally, he spoke.

"You know, police in the Ozarks aren't like the ones in the city. They don't have the same rules or the same motivation that a city cop might have. The crimes they encounter down here are probably pretty small compared to what you might see in the city. Life goes at a slower pace. People know and trust each other down here. They like to give others the benefit of doubt, with the belief that most people are good at heart and will do the right thing without too much motivation. I can understand why the police might have given those kids the benefit of the doubt. They got drunk and said something they shouldn't have. A fight broke out a gun was fired. Nothing too sinister about that. Even the drugs that were taken wouldn't have put up much of a red flag. Meth was starting to get common in the Ozarks at about that time. They had a decent quantity of it but not enough to be suspicious of them dealing drugs. I can understand that the gun and the meth might have got misplaced and may have even gotten thrown out. But what I do have difficulty understanding is why there wasn't a greater effort to find those two men, particularly after what happened over the course of the next three weeks."

"Geez, Booger. Please, just tell me what happened," I said, showing a bit of frustration in my voice.

"Patience, son, I'm getting to it."

I didn't mean to show my frustration. Booger was, from what I could tell, a damn good private eye, with a good heart and even better intentions. But crap, he talked in circles and never seemed to draw any conclusions. I knew what he was saying about stating the facts. I had always admired reporters, and if I was ever going to be one, I'd need to state the facts. But as someone who was trying to get the big picture here, it was frustrating. No one was closer to these facts than, perhaps, Harley himself. Wasn't I the one researching here? Isn't Booger my source? I wanted my source to tell me what I thought. This whole thing felt more and more like an award-winning article I could get published. And so I wanted this cowboy detective in the red hot rod to say something.

"I'll be patient," I told him. "I just want you to tell me as much as you can."

As soon as I said those words, I regretted them. What was I asking for? Rose was right when she said he had a gift for gab. He had been talking all day now. My back was aching, my ass was glued to the seat, and I had a huge headache from all the coffee and second-hand cigar smoke I'd taken in. It was past 8 p.m. now. I was beginning to wonder what time the diner closed.

"It was the next day, I believe," Booger continued, "that the Springfield police discovered that Rachael had been sitting in the county jail just a few miles away. Of course, by the time they discovered that she was gone. So were her two friends.

"The fact that local authorities released everyone

without being interrogated had to be embarrassing. Add to that were the questions about a city attorney from way up in Kansas City coming down to represent three rednecks that didn't appear to have a pot to piss in. Why was he there? Who hired him? Who paid for him? Then mix in a license plate that was stolen, the gun that had no serial number, and the fake names and addresses that the two men gave. To say the good old boy city and county police were embarrassed was an understatement. They were pissed.

"The police had no idea where to find the two men," he said. "But they sure as hell had an idea where to look for Rachael. Becky told them she was living in Gary's trailer in Nixa.

"And guess what? Suddenly the cops figured out how to work together again because Springfield and Nixa boys visited Gary's mother's trailer. And, you know, they knocked, but no one answered, so they did what every blue-blooded, redneck, small-town sheriff dreams of doing when they are armed with a search warrant, and no one answers the door, they kicked it in.

"Damn, I wish that I would have been there. I've always wanted to do that," Booger said with the gleeful smile of a child on Christmas morning.

"Inside the trailer, they found Rachael. She was dead, a drug overdose, it looked like, and it was later confirmed in an autopsy. Meth was found on the table next to her, and a large quantity of it was discovered in her body during the autopsy."

"In the bedroom, they found Mrs. Walker, Gary's mother. She was dead too. An oxygen tank next to her bed was empty, and her breathing tube had been removed. The coroner ruled that her death was the result of natural causes. She was, after all, a sickly elderly woman, completely dependent on her supply of oxygen.

"I did find something curious about Mrs. Walker's death," he said, taking another sip of coffee.

Damn, Booger McLain, I remember thinking. He had told me half of this before, but this was his M.O. He'd take me to some dead end in his story and then veer off-road to a whole new destination. It felt like he was toying with me.

"There was another oxygen tank, a completely full one, against the wall in her room, about five feet from her bed. From reading the police reports, there didn't appear to be any attempt to hook her breathing tube up to that full tank."

See, I was right. "Wow. I knew she ran out of oxygen, but you're saying she seriously had another tank?" I said. "Maybe she was unable to get to it? You had said before that she was completely bedridden. Maybe she needed help to reach the tank and hook it up?"

"Maybe?" Booger said with a look that told me he had more to say. "I read in the police report that she had fresh, unsoiled pajamas when she was found," Booger continued.

"Odd thing is that if she was completely bedridden, how did she change clothes, and how did she get to the bathroom to relieve herself? The police found her, and the coroner that picked her body up didn't mention a smell of urine."

"So?" I asked.

"Son, have you ever been in a nursing home? Around really old people that can't do anything for themselves?"

"No."

"Well, let me tell you, they always smell like urine, even after putting on a fresh set of pajamas. It's a smell that just sticks around. Wait until you're older son and you start pissing your pants. You'll see. That urine smell will never leave you."

"So, are you saying something sinister happened to Mrs. Walker because she was wearing clean pajamas and didn't reek of urine?" I asked.

"No, I'm not saying that. Don't put words in my mouth, son. All I'm saying is that I found it a little odd, that's all."

"What about Rachael?" I asked. "Did you find anything odd about her death?"

"Well, now that you mention it. There was one thing," he replied. "It was the meth that they found on the table next to her body."

"OK, what was odd about that?" I asked, taking Booger's bait.

"Well, it was blue, crystal meth, which is unusual.

I found that the kind Harley has shared with people—you know, to get 'em hooked—was pinkish. Mostly white. But blue is the same type of meth that the police confiscated from the van, from Rachael and those two men."

"Okay. So, it was looking like Harley had maybe murdered Rachael and Gary's mother, but do you think now it was possibly the two men that were with Rachael when she was arrested?' I asked, doubting I'd get an answer. "Or maybe, both the men and Harley were involved?"

Booger ignored my questions and continued.

"You know, another curious thing is the amount of meth discovered by the police on that table."

I was desperately hoping that Booger was leading toward some type of conclusion.

"The quantity of meth the police reported finding on the table in Mrs. Walker's trailer was two ounces, the same amount of blue meth the county police found in the van and the same quantity of meth that disappeared from the police evidence room."

CHAPTER 13
LOSING IT ALL

Booger sat back in the booth, lifted his coffee mug halfway to his face and stopped. He was staring out the front window of the diner. It looked like he was frozen in place. It was dark outside, raining now, hard. The sound of the rain colliding with the glass window made a loud echo that vibrated throughout the nearly empty diner. A light fog had crept up, causing the diner's windows to blur. It was impossible to see more than a few inches past that glass window. I had no idea what he was looking at.

For a few seconds, I thought maybe he had entered some sort of caffeine-induced coma. God knows he had drunk enough coffee that day to kill a lesser man.

Suddenly, he snapped out of it and returned to his

coffee mug.

"The next part is what I don't understand, what I will never understand," Booger continued. "Up until this point, there had been no truly innocent victims to this story. Yeah, maybe you can make an argument that Steve was an innocent person, but he had an idea of the danger he was walking into when he drove Gary down to do the money drop. But that baby was. Innocent, that is. She had no choice in what happened to her. What unfolded was a true tragedy."

His seriousness caught me off guard. Yes, he was dramatic, but this seemed more like the detective being lost for words, which was out of character.

Booger paused again and gained his composure. I could see the lump in his throat. I could see he was fighting not to show his emotions.

"Becky Jacobs was a good person. She would have made an even better mother. That, of course, is only my opinion from people I talked to and information I knew about her. She never purposely hurt anyone. No one had an unkind word to say about her. Yeah, she considered abortion. Maybe some people would say that just considering it meant she wasn't the sweet, kind-hearted girl that others made her out to be. But I didn't feel that way. Having a baby that young, without a husband, without the financial means to take good care of the baby, and with the hopes of aspirations of getting a college education being put on indefinite hold to support a baby, I think a lot of girls would consider alternatives."

"Ultimately, though, she made the right decision to give birth," he said. "Again, my opinion: hearing the heartbeat of her little girl seemed to change everything," Booger added. "Becky showed it to the Raymonds after Steve's body was found in Lake Honor. Did she tell you that?" he asked me.

"Yes, she showed it to me."

I didn't tell Booger that Dorothy had given me the little picture labeled "Emma," that the losses in her life were too raw, too hurtful to be reminded of the picture of her granddaughter lying contently in her mother's womb, unaware of the tragedies still to come.

"That picture of her daughter opened up an entirely new chapter in her life. She was excited to become a mother. Her friends and her family saw a change in her, a glow, an enthusiasm they had not seen for a long time. Her mother mistook it as young love. Maybe Steve had come back into her life, or maybe she had found someone new.

"Becky never told her parents about the baby. The first time they found out about her pregnancy was when the accident occurred. It seemed odd to me that she hadn't told her mother in particular about the baby. They appeared to be very close. Maybe she planned to and just hadn't reached that point yet. Maybe she was afraid they would be disappointed. The dreams of becoming a nurse or doctor, of getting a college education, of being financially secure would all be put on hold for this baby."

"So, tell me about the accident, about what happened to Becky and her baby?" I asked. The diner was completely empty of customers now. It was getting late.

"A few days after the bodies of Rachael and Gary's mother were discovered in the trailer, Becky had an unexpected visitor.

"It was late at night. Becky was getting ready for bed when someone knocked on the door. From what I was told, she didn't answer it at first. It was late at night, after all, and she wasn't expecting any visitors. But the knocking persisted. So, after a while, she went to the door, but she didn't open it, not at first anyway. She kept the door locked and asked from the inside of the door who was there and what did they wanted?

"It was a lady's voice that responded. The visitor told Becky that she had information about Steve. Becky opened the door. Based on what she would tell Dorothy later, the woman was young, maybe twenty. She wore a lot of make-up and a bright, colorful tube top and black miniskirt. She supposedly looked like a hooker, or what Becky imagined a hooker to look like. There was something else too. Her eyes were large and glassy, as if she was on something.

"She handed Becky a piece of paper. On it was a hand-drawn map, the number 40 and a time, midnight.

"Those were the only things on the paper. She would

later show it to the police," he said. "The unknown visitor told Becky that Steve was alive, that he was being held captive because he owed a lot of money. The 40 written on the note was short for $40,000, the amount of money the girl told Becky that Steve owed, the amount of money it would take to get him back.

"The map was where Becky needed to deliver the money. The time written on the note, midnight, was when the money needed to be delivered the very next night. 'Don't contact the police. Come by yourself' was the last instruction the stranger gave Becky," he said.

"After giving Becky the note and message, the girl left quickly. Becky was shaken. Her first thought, her only thought right then, was to talk to the Raymonds. They needed to hear the news about their son. They, too, had his best interest in mind. Maybe they would have some idea of what to do.

"It was late. The Raymonds were sound asleep when Becky arrived at their door. She rang the doorbell several times until she saw the light come on in the hallway leading to the front door. She was crying uncontrollably and shaking when Earl opened the door.

"We don't know exactly what was said between Becky and the Raymonds, but we do have police reports and statements that Dorothy and Earl Raymond made later that give us their side.

"Dorothy said that it took a couple of cups of hot tea

and about twenty minutes to calm Becky down enough so they could understand what had happened. They said she showed them the note. She told them exactly what the visitor had told her and the instructions she had been given for the money drop.

"'I think we need to call the police,' Earl remembered telling her.

"But Becky was adamant that was not the thing to do. She had been told to come alone. She had been instructed not to contact the police. Becky was certain that whoever had kidnapped Steve and Gary would surely hurt them, maybe even kill them if the police were involved."

"So, what did the Raymonds do?" I asked.

"They assured Becky that everything would be OK, and by they, I mean Dorothy. She was the rock of the family, the one that was most level-headed. Dorothy comforted Becky and told her that they would come up with the money and they would not involve the police.

"Earl was not in agreement with his wife. He wanted to get the police involved from the minute Becky walked in the front door. They would know the way to handle this, he thought. They would protect his son. But his wife was making promises to Becky. The parents were like two roosters in a hen house, and the chicken wire would hold."

"Wait. What? So, who got their way, Earl or Dorothy?" I asked.

"Both of them, actually," Booger responded.

"Earl stayed quiet that night, leaving Dorothy and Becky to think he was in agreement with their plan to keep the police out of the loop. He even arranged to get the money, all $40,000 from savings, his retirement. You know, that's a lot of scratch," Booger said, still smiling from the joke before.

"Neither Dorothy nor Becky was aware that he had reached out to the cops. He told the detective he spoke with no one was aware he'd gone to the police, that they were unwilling to cooperate and wouldn't want to drop the money if they knew.

"$40,000 was just about every dime the Raymonds had to their name. Earl had borrowed against his retirement account. The detective had assured him that they would recover the money, that his team would have eyes on the ransom the entire time and that whoever picked it up would be arrested immediately."

Booger smiled and took another sip of coffee, "Got to love small-town police. They're writing checks with no money in their account. They thought they were dealing with some dim-whited hillbilly out to make a quick buck, or $40,000 quick bucks in this case, and had no idea of the creek he was up with no paddle.

"The police had a good idea that Harley was behind the ransom demand. It seems all crooked roads lead to Harley. Or at least this one, right? I mean, what're the odds? They had already been told about the letter left in Billy Bob's for Rachael. You know, the one that asked for $40,000. Rachael said that was Harley's demand. Then, there was the fire at Rachael's house, the one ruled to be caused by arson. Rachael was convinced that Harley was the one that was behind that fire. She told the police that. Then, there was the fire at Billy Bob's not long after that letter was left with the bartender. There was speculation that Harley started that fire, too, although arson investigators were conflicted on whether the fire was a result of arson or an electrical problem.

"Anyway, there were just too many coincidences to think Harley wasn't involved. So, they were certainly anxious to catch him picking up that money. Then they could arrest him and, one way or another, get the truth out of him, maybe resolve several open cases along the way.

"But there was one big problem that they hadn't taken into consideration," Booger said and then took a long pause waiting for me to ask what that problem was.

"What was the problem," I finally asked.

"The police had no fuck'n idea who Harley was. They didn't know his real name. They didn't know his background. They didn't know what he was capable of. They thought they were swatting a fly and wound up knock'n down a hornet's nest.

"So, anyways, back to the money," Booger said. "Earl got it, all $40,000 in cash. Kid, have you ever seen that much cash in twenty-dollar bills? There was so much that it wouldn't fit in a normal bag. He had to use a pillowcase to put it all in.

"The police screwed up in so many ways, and the money was one of 'em. Looking back from the rearview mirror, it's easy to say they should have involved the FBI from the very beginning. They didn't. They claimed later that there just wasn't enough time. By the time Earl notified them, there were only about twelve hours remaining before the money drop needed to take place. That, of course, was bullshit. The minute they thought those two boys had been kidnapped, they should have contacted the FBI. But they didn't.

"If there's one Achilles heel of people from the Ozarks, it's that they think they can handle their own problems. It's a mentality I find in our folks. They just simply don't want to ask for help.

"The money was a missed opportunity. It should have been marked. The serial numbers should have been recorded. They could have tracked the money if it got into the wrong hands. They didn't do that. Maybe they were so confident that Harley would never get his hands on that money that they didn't consider options if he did."

"Oh no, Booger. Please tell me Harley didn't get away with Earl and Dorothy's $40,000?" I asked. I could see where this was going, and the coffee cowboy was enjoying himself way too much for it to be anywhere good. "What happened with the money drop?"

"Well, it went over exactly as planned," he said, smiling and holding a pause for dramatic effect, "or that's what everyone seemed to think.

"Becky showed up at the drop with the pillowcase of money. She left it right at the spot that was indicated on the map she was given. She waited for nearly an hour, hoping to see someone pick up the pillowcase, hoping to see Steve and Gary. But no one showed up. The pillowcase was never touched. There had been no instructions about what she was supposed to do after she dropped off the money. The note had been void of any details, and the visitor that had given it to her was vague, or maybe she was just high and forgot to tell her what to do next.

"Anyway, after an hour, she drove away and headed back south toward Springfield. She didn't make it very far, though. All hell broke out after she left.

"A combination of Springfield police, county police and the state police, about a dozen officers and plain clothed detectives had taken up positions completely around the drop area, in the hills above, but close enough they could see everything that was going on around that pillowcase. They saw Becky's car leave. A few minutes later, gunfire broke out in the hills around them, lots of gunfire, hundreds of rounds, they estimated later. It was like a war zone, with gunfire erupting everywhere around them, but there was no sign of the enemy that was firing on them. Then, as rapidly as the gunfire had erupted around them, it stopped just as suddenly. No one had been shot. But those cops, sure as hell, took cover, and in the confusion, that pillowcase of money disappeared.

"No one heard the car go off the road, down a large hill and stop after hitting a large oak tree. Additional police alerted by the frantic calls for help by their fellow officers, came upon the accident just a mile north of the drop-off.

"Becky Jacobs was lucky. She survived that accident. Her daughter did not."

"Was it an accident?" I asked.

"The police didn't know. There was a lot of confusion after the gunfire started. Becky heard it when she was only a few hundred yards down the road. She thought someone was shooting at her. She sped up. The roads in those parts were treacherous, especially at night, especially to someone that hadn't traveled them before. Becky told police that she was traveling fast and that as she entered a sharp turn in the road, a truck coming the other way nearly collided with her. She felt a loss of control as she came out of the turn, and the car went off the road and down the hill, crashing into the tree."

"Sounds like an accident to me," I replied.

"Yeah, but there were a couple of things curious about that accident," Booger replied.

"Like what?"

"Hey, honey," Booger yelled to the waitress behind the counter. She was cleaning up. There were no customers in the diner now. It was nearly 10pm. "What's your name?"

"Margo," she replied. "Margo, sweetie, can you bring us some fresh coffee.

"Don't have any, hun. We close in an hour, and the only coffee we got left has been sitting for a couple of hours."

"That's OK, Margo. We'll take two cups of that, as long as it's hot."

"So, what did you find curious about Becky's accident?" I asked.

"Well, first, her left, rear tire was flat when the police arrived."

"So, it probably was flattened on the way down that embankment after she lost control of the car."

"Yeah, that's exactly what the police thought too.

"Odd thing is," Booger continued, "Her daddy had just bought four brand new tires for that car to keep his little girl safe. But I suppose even a brand-new tire can get a flat if it hits or runs over the right thing. But, then again, the state trooper that was first on the scene of the accident described the hole in the tire as about the size of a ping pong ball with rubber chard pieces slicing outward from the hole. He noted that the only time he had seen that type of damage before was from a rifle blast."

"Shit, so you think someone was trying to kill her," I asked.

"No, I didn't say that. Fact is the police figured the

roads, weather and her speeding resulted in that crash."

"You mentioned two things that bothered you about the accident. What was the other?" I asked.

"Well, it was the truck, the one that Becky nearly hit, coming around the corner just before she lost control. It was discovered the next day, in daylight, when a tow truck arrived to take the car away, that there was blue paint and a dent on the rear left side of Becky's car. The police assumed the truck she met coming around the corner must have grazed her car. She lost control immediately after. Whoever was driving that pickup truck must have seen her go off the road and down the hill. But they didn't stop, and no one called the police to report the accident.

"There's probably nothing to it. The driver might have been drinking or had some other reason not to alert the police. Maybe he figured someone else would be along shortly to attend to whoever was in the car, or maybe he simply didn't hear the screeching of her tires or the sounds of her car rolling down the mountain behind him. Hell, anything is possible. It's just a bit out of character for hill people to not help someone that is in trouble.

"It didn't matter. The truck driver, the accident, and the lost money seemed pretty unimportant with the news of that baby's death. Becky was devastated. Her parents and Steve's parents were too. No one even knew about the baby except for Becky. Suddenly she had to explain that Steve Raymond was the father. She had to explain why she hadn't told anyone about the baby, not even Steve.

"He was gone now, taken, kidnapped for $40,000 that was ultimately paid. But, still no, Steve. Everyone was thinking the worst, but no one was talking about it. The police had fucked up. They had underestimated the criminals they were dealing with. Yeah, now they knew that they were dealing with a group of bad guys, not just Harley. This wasn't like any group of moonshining or pot-growing hillbillies they had ever encountered before. They were smart, organized and camouflaged somewhere within those deep, dense Ozark woods where finding them would take a miracle."

CHAPTER 14
CLOSING TIME

"What happened to Becky after her baby died?" I asked.

"She grieved, I suppose," Booger said, staring out the window into the dark streets illuminated in soft, gold patches by streetlights. For the first time, he looked tired to me. "Not long after that, the bodies of those two boys floated to the top of Lake Honor.

"Then the Raymonds and the Jacobs grieved together," he said. "That was also when Becky and Dorothy got really close. That's when they needed each other the most.

"It's also when Earl's health began to deteriorate. He never would admit it, but I think he blamed himself for what happened to his son and Becky's baby."

"Was that because he contacted the police and got

them involved?" I asked.

"Yeah, it would appear. From what others said about him, Earl had always been very strong-minded. He believed in doing the right thing, conforming to rules and believing the police always did the right thing. He had never had a need for the help of the police before. Now he needed them, and even though his wife refused to accept their help, he was determined to seek it. He truly believed they knew what they were doing, that they would get his son back and that they would bring those boy's kidnappers to justice.

"He was devastated at what happened that night at the drop, and when news came that his son was one of the bodies in the lake, he withdrew, I guess. Inside himself. He was tired."

"What about Dorothy? How did she handle it all?"

"How would any mother handle news of the murder of her only child?" Booger asked in a tone that told me how stupid a question that was.

Booger took another sip of coffee, tasting it and spitting it back into his cup. "Damn, it's cold. Flo, honey, get us two more refills."

"My name's Margo," she replied.

"Sorry, Margo. You look like a Flo to me. Has anyone ever told you that?"

"No one who was sober," she replied.

"Margo, can you get us a couple of refills?"

"Sorry, hun. Coffee's gone. We close in twenty minutes. Can I get you something else before we close? We still have a couple of donuts left."

"No thanks, sweetie. Just bring the check.

"So, what were we talking about?" he asked, looking at me.

"You were talking about Dorothy and Earl after the death of their son?"

"Oh yeah. Well, like I was saying, both Earl and Dorothy didn't take it well. And they both handled their grief differently. Earl held everything inside. From all accounts, he refused to talk about his son's death. Maybe it was guilt, probably it was guilt, but I think it was more than that. I think his faith in people was gone. It seemed a part of him died the day his son was found. Sometimes people give up. Who knows, really, but I think he gave up that day, that he stopped caring about life."

Booger was speculating. He was saying something. He was sharing his thoughts, however meekly. He must have been tired.

"His health went downhill after that," Booger said. "He quit his job and retired early. He rarely left the house anymore, talked, or got out of his chair in the living room.

"Dorothy became the rock of the family. She and Becky became close. They leaned on each other for support.

"Dorothy was the one that contacted me, desperate

to uncover exactly what happened to her son," Booger said. "The police were no help. Maybe after the fiasco at the money drop, they were afraid, or maybe they just didn't care, chalking whatever had occurred to those boys up to hill justice. That would be easier.

"We know the cause of those boy's deaths was ruled an accident. When it comes to kids of their ages, there are three types of accidental deaths in the Ozarks: drowning, car accidents, and drug overdoses. This story has all three, and it wasn't done yet," he said, perking up a bit. He seemed to have caught a second wind. "It's damn easy for the police to sweep any death under the carpet if it's an accident, so they don't need to do any real police work. I've often wondered how many of those so-called accidental deaths were really the result of some sort of perverted idea of hill justice.

"Dorothy contacted me when she had no one else to turn to. In hindsight, I probably shouldn't have taken her money. I probably shouldn't have told her that I would help. I knew from the beginning what I was up against, that I would never be able to bring the boy's killers to justice."

"Maybe, she didn't care about justice," I said. "Maybe she just wanted answers to what happened to her son?"

Booger leaned back in the booth, looking directly at me as if pondering my answer. I should have known better.

"What, are you some sort of psychiatrist? A city-boy psychic, perhaps?" He replied in his usual sarcastic tone. "No, she wanted justice. I'm certain of that. That's why I never took any more of her money. That's why I eventually stopped providing her weekly updates. It was just too painful for her to give her more details about her son but not be told that I was any closer to bringing her what she needed. Before there can be justice, there has to be proof. And more than that, the cops have to believe its proof. And the cops wanted this thing to go away."

"I've got to ask you, Booger, if this whole thing wasn't an accident, then it had to be murder, right? Don't you think they were murdered?"

"Don't you dare print a fuck'n word of this, do you hear me?" he said in a threatening tone.

"I won't. I promise."

"Yes, I'm certain they were murdered. There were just too many things that happened to support that. Hell, almost anyone that was involved or got involved in the initial robbery of Harley in the park and the money drop afterward either found themselves dead or suffered some other loss."

"So, do you think Harley was the murderer?" I asked.

"I don't know. I definitely think that he was involved, but to what extent, I don't know?"

"What makes you think others were involved?" I asked.

"Well, the lawyer from Kansas City that came down to get the charges dropped for Rachael and those two guys is one clue that others were involved. Who called that lawyer? It sure as hell wasn't Rachael or the two rednecks she was with. They hadn't called anyone since their arrest, according to police records. So, who even knew they were sitting in jail?

"There was something else, too," Booger said before being interrupted.

"Here's your check, boys," the waitress said, putting it down on the table. "It's closing time."

"Thanks, Flo," Booger replied.

"It's Margo," she replied.

"Sorry, sweetie. Did I tell you how much you remind me of a Flo I once knew?"

Margo just walked away, not saying a word.

"Well, I guess it's time to leave, son. They'll be turning the lights out on us soon."

"But I've still got a lot of questions for you, Booger," I said in a tone that was somewhere between desperation and exasperation. I had been so tired. I wanted to leave at least two hours ago, and Booger kept me hanging on. Now, we were at the finish line, and he wanted to quit. And I didn't want to leave. I think he could see it in my face.

"Well, son, it's a ten-minute drive to your motel. I suggest you ask me what you want to ask on the way."

The bill was for less than ten dollars. Booger threw down a twenty, and we walked out of the diner. As we walked away and got into his car, I decided to prioritize my questions, knowing that, at best, I would get answers to only two or three of them during that ten-minute ride.

"Booger, what happened to Becky?"

"Well, she died, kid. It was shortly after she stopped talking to Dorothy. Those two just got tired of talking about Steve, I guess. Too damn painful. They drifted apart, and shortly after, Becky died of an overdose. She was found in her apartment, doors locked. Her parents had tried to contact her for two days without success, so they called the police. The landlord had to let them in. Like I said, the doors were locked. She was found face down in her bed, fully clothed, with a small quantity of Ozark coke lying next to her."

"White meth or blue meth?" I asked.

"The police report didn't say. Her death was determined to be accidental."

"Was anyone aware that she had a drug problem?" I asked.

"No, the curious thing was that no one that knew her was aware that she took any sort of drugs. Hell, she didn't even drink. But I guess there's a first for everything?"

"You don't really think she took those drugs willingly, do you, Booger?"

"Doesn't matter what I think. The evidence supported an accidental death. The only door leading into the apartment was locked from the inside. All the windows were locked, too, except for one in her bedroom. The police dusted it for fingerprints, but Becky's were the only fingerprints found."

We were getting close to my motel now. I only had time for one or two more questions.

"Those two guys that were with Rachael in the van, did you ever find out who they were?"

"No, I didn't, son. There was something curious that happened not long after those two boys' bodies were found in Lake Honor."

"What was that?" I asked.

"Well, two rednecks drown in Lake Taneycomo. Two young lovers that were there getting some alone time, if you know what I mean, reported seeing a van pull up near the lake on a seldom used gravel road. They were too far away to see who was in the van. A few minutes later, they heard the sound of something being thrown in or falling into the water. They didn't think anything of it. Maybe a couple of kids, drunk or high, decided to go for a late-night swim. It was a little past midnight. A little while later, they heard the van's engine start up and drive away back down the gravel road."

"Did they notice the color of the van? I asked.

"No, they said it was too dark, and the van didn't have its lights on."

"What about that gravel road? Where did it lead to?"

"That's another curious thing, son. According to the couple, the only place they could think it went to was to the backside of the School of the Ozarks."

"Shit," I said.

"Oh, don't get excited, son. I went down to the spot where those rednecks' bodies were found. The water patrol that picked them up figured their bodies didn't travel too far, not that time of the year. The water was calm. There wasn't any boat traffic, and there wasn't much of a current. I interviewed the two lovers that were there. They took me to the spot they were that night. They took me to the gravel road where the van was parked. I followed that gravel road all the way back. About a mile away, the road split. One way led to the dairy on the campus of S of O. The other road wound around through some farm country before connecting with another road that led directly into the town of Hollister."

"So, there is no way of knowing if that van went to S of O or Hollister?" I asked.

"That's right, son. But there was someone else that was curious about those rednecks' death."

Oh no, I thought. *Here we go again. He led me to another dead end and was taking me off-road. And we didn't have a lot of time.*

"Well, there were actually two curious things. First, their bodies were found fully clothed. Odd going swimming in the Lake in early November. Even odder, do it fully clothed. Add to that those boys had not one single piece of identity on them."

"So, were they ever identified?" I asked.

"The police ran the fingerprints of both boys. One came back as a small-time criminal that had served six months for theft. I believe his name was Darryl. I don't recall his last name. The other fingerprint did not lead to anyone in the police database."

"A run of Darryl's social security number showed that he was last employed at the Dairy on the campus of S of O. Further investigation discovered that he and another man by the name of Homer Collins had just simply run off on the same day, five days before the two bodies were discovered. They left without telling anyone. They left without collecting their last paycheck."

"Damn," I said.

We had pulled into the motel lot now, and Booger had stopped the car directly in front of my room.

"OK, you're home, kid," he said.

"Wait, I said. You've got to answer one more question, Booger."

"I don't gotta do nothing, son, but I'm feeling generous. Hit me one last time."

"You told me earlier that you were nearly killed, and that's how you found out the identity of Harley. Tell me about it."

"Well, now, I may have been blowing smoke up your nose just a little bit. I never, for certain, knew Harley's real name. I had the misfortune of coming face to face with him, but it wasn't exactly a cordial conversation where we introduced each other. I was driving back from S of O after interviewing those two lovers and after following the gravel road where the van was parked. I decided to take the scenic route back, highway 110, the same road that was taken for the money drop, the same road that claimed the life of Becky's baby.

"It was starting to get dark by the time I left the school. By the time I was on highway 110, it was completely dark except for a full moon that was shining that night. That road is narrow with hairpin turns. It was also completely deserted. That was until I came around a bend, and a pick-up truck appeared from nowhere behind me, right on my fucking bumper. On a short flataway, the truck passed me. A few seconds later, another pick-up came up from behind, right on my bumper. That's when the truck in front of me slowed down, and the truck behind locked bumpers with mine. A third truck came around on my left. Two guys, faces covered, were in the truck. Their passenger window rolled down, and a shotgun was pointed directly at me. 'Follow the truck ahead of you if you want to see another day,' the passenger said.

"Now, I'm not one to scare, but I was curious about what they had to show, so I did as I was told and followed the truck down the road about two hundred yards, then onto a dirt road. We followed that dirt road for about two miles, then it turned onto a narrow path in the woods in the middle of nowhere.

"When the truck stopped. Two large guys, faces covered, pulled me out of my car and dragged me to a tall oak tree about twenty yards away. I let 'em think they're getting the best of me, so, you know, they beat me up real nice, and I didn't fight too hard. For knowledge, kid," he said before powering through. "Anyhow, I thought maybe, possibly, my life was going to be over that night. That's because as I lay on the ground bleeding, one guy, the leader, I assumed, bent down to me with a large hunting knife. He put the blades of the knife against my throat with his right hand while holding a beer in his left.

"I hear that you are looking for me," he said, taking a final drink from a nearly empty can of beer before squashing it flat and throwing it on the ground. "City boy, the funny thing is that everyone that comes looking for me winds up looking a little bit like that can of beer. It was good imagery.

"I could tell from his voice, from the look in his eyes, that I was dealing with a psycho. I knew he was giving me one warning, and that was going to be the only warning I would get. I would need to drop my investigation or suffer the fate of Steve, Gary, Rachael and Becky. It's the Icarus problem. Have you heard of Icarus?"

"Yes, well, yeah," I said, struggling to remember my religious theory class from the year before.

"Yeah, well, Icarus flew too close to the sun—I think he

was an investigator, too—and he got burned real nice."

I was pretty sure Professor Jones had described it differently.

"I chose to stop the investigation that night," Booger said. "I never traveled down Highway 110 again."

"But how did you discover Harley's real name?"

"Son, you're mistaken. I never discovered his real name. Someone sent a letter to the FBI, an anonymous source. They described an encounter with Harley where he threatened their life. That anonymous person gave a description of the truck Harley was driving along with the license plate. They even sent a flattened can of beer with the letter advising the FBI to check the fingerprints on the can.

"It was that anonymous source that helped the FBI determine the real identity of Harley."

"OK, so it wasn't you. But I know you mentioned that his name was Michael or something. Anyway, what did the FBI discover about his identity?"

"Son, it doesn't matter anymore. Hell, nothing about this story matters anymore. Nobody cares."

"You and I care, and I figure Dorothy and Earl care too."

"Well, you're a fool, and I am too, and so are the Raymonds. Nobody gives a damn, trust me."

I couldn't understand it. Why had he spent all day telling me this full story at great length and detail just to end here? It didn't make sense. He really didn't seem the type to scare easily. Was he all bluster? What was I missing? "Will you at least tell me if the police ever caught up with Harley?"

"Yeah, they caught up to him, alright. He was dead, a drug overdose, they said."

"Umm, okay. What about the meth business he had?"

"Gone, but not gone," Booger replied.

"What do you mean?"

"Exactly what I said. The FBI found his drug lab, but all the drugs were gone, most of the equipment too. They never did find out what happened to it. But you know what, kid?"

He spoke before I could answer. "This meth, or speed or crank or Ozarks' coke—whatever you want to call it—is stronger than ever in these parts, now. More people die every day from overdoses. Someone is supplying the product, and on a much larger scale than ever before, but the police can never seem to find the source. The manufacture and distribution of the product is much more sophisticated now, after Harley's death. It seems locals took over the operation. Filled whatever gap the death of Harley left.

"Son, it's almost as if it's become big business. Like it's hiding in plain sight. But not all questions get answered. Especially if outsiders are the ones asking," and he smiled. And he turned to leave.

I tried to get him to say more, but Booger was done talking. He shook my hand, wished me a good life, and drove off. I would never see him again.

CHAPTER 15
THE STORY

When I returned to the motel, I wrote down as much of what Booger had told me while it was still fresh in my mind. There was one more place I needed to visit, and then I felt I'd be ready to write the story. I still didn't know just what I would write or exactly who I was writing this for. I had thought, if it was good enough, maybe it could be in the Kansas City Star or St. Louis Post-Dispatch. Who knows? Maybe one day it could be a book, I thought. Maybe it could lead to a career. What mattered, above all else, was finding some closure, an ending to it all.

The morning after my day with Booger, my destination was the deepest, densest part of the Ozarks, the secluded drop-off site on Highway 110. The landscape changed about twenty minutes south of Springfield, and it felt like you were entering a lost world. The hills started down, dropping from the plateau and then rose again. Three turns off the main thoroughfare, Highway 65, was where I began the trek on Highway 110. It was a narrow, two-lane road with hairpin turns just like Booger had described it. The road straddled Stone and Taney county lines through areas of the Ozarks that seemed still undiscovered by civilization. The road was paved but probably not for many years. It seemed every road that met it was gravel or dirt—and indistinguishable from rural driveways. The white line that separated the southbound and northbound lanes was faded and nearly impossible to see in some spots. I found myself praying I wouldn't meet a large semi-truck coming in the opposite direction.

This was an unnerving, wild place for me, a boy from Kansas City. I'd been in the bad areas of KC before but never felt so anxious. In the poorest, most crime-filled parts of Kansas City, there were people you could see under streetlights. Someone could be ten feet away in the remote Ozarks, and you might never see them. This was the camouflaged state. This was a part of southern Missouri that was seen as a gaping white hole in the nationwide cell phone coverage maps. This was camping country where you'd better stick to the trails and bring bear spray. This is where one could see a billion stars at night through a hillside clearing, but it's also a place of strange codes. On 110 that day, I saw a bright blue-

painted rock pointing out from a hill at the start of a curve
and a brown-straw scarecrow hanging from a tree. Heading
into one turn, I saw a large, plastic owl duct-taped to a branch
facing the road. That message seemed clear: we see you.

There were orange-lettered Private Property and
Do-Not-Enter signs at the end of gravel driveways next to
mailboxes with shotguns carved into wood stands. This
wasn't like sparsely populated sections of central western
Kansas where you could see an oncoming car from miles
away. This was thick, suffocating foliage all around, and it
was often dark even in the daytime under the canopy of trees.
I was full of nerves the whole time I was driving, wondering
what could pop up around the next turn or over the crest of
the next hill, wondering who was watching me and who I
might be failing to see.

I couldn't even imagine trying to navigate that road at
night without the benefit of sunlight. Even in daylight, it took
all my awareness to keep me on the highway.

There were few road signs, no speed limit signs that I
could see. There was no need for them. If you wanted to live,
you drove slowly.

I had come to see it for myself, to feel what Steve, Gary
and Becky had experienced on their fateful trips down it, the
fear, the darkness, the anxiousness. But I had also come to say
goodbye to them, yes, but also to the Ozarks that I had grown
to both love and hate in such a short period of time.

From what Booger had told me, I had a good idea where Becky's car had left the roadway when it fell down the mountain and collided with that thick oak tree. From that spot, I knew the money drop off, the last place Steve and Gary had gone willingly, was only a mile south.

I had heard that a cross was left to mark the area where Becky's accident had occurred. I was hopeful of finding that cross. I had even brought flowers to lay next to it. But the deeper I got into the Ozarks, I realized finding that cross would not be easy. The highway was littered with crosses. That road had been the cause of countless accidents and countless deaths over the years. There were crosses marking those spots everywhere on both sides of the highway. I remember realizing how it might be that the sheriff in Branson could be dismissive of a car ending up at the bottom of a steep embankment.

I did find a cross, a simple one, made from two narrow branches of a tree. It was in the general area that I understood Becky's car to leave the road. The cross had no flowers, not even wilted ones that had been left long ago. There was no name, no indication for whom the cross was placed. It may not have been the baby's cross. It didn't matter. Whoever's cross it was had died before their time, lonely, afraid, just like Becky's baby. I said the Lord's prayer and left the flowers.

From there, I drove a mile south to a small clearing off the road. This, I was certain, was where Steve, Gary and

Becky had gone to drop off the money. The clearing was in a valley between two mountains. I imagined the police sitting high above the drop zone, watching and waiting for someone to pick up that pillowcase of money. They would be completely hidden at night amongst the tall oak trees and dense wilderness. So, who were the people that fired a bombardment of gunshots to get their attention away from that pillowcase? Whoever fired those shots had no interest in shooting anyone. Hell, they probably couldn't even see the officers that were scattered throughout the woods. The gunfire had to be a distraction, a way to take the pillowcase of money without being noticed.

Did the gunfire play a part in Becky's accident? I wondered. *Or was it the pick-up truck she encountered on the road? Did the flat tire that was found on her car cause her to lose control? And, was the flat tire the result of a rifle shot or some sort of natural cause?*

I was coming to the realization those questions would never be answered.

There were no crosses to mark where those boys met their fate. I kneeled down where I was, facing the green-and-shadowed hillside, and said a prayer.

Then I got in my car and headed home.

There were so many details, so much information, that I poured over in the following weeks. It was a huge chore to condense it all into a marketable newspaper story, but I managed it somehow. I stuck to the facts and left all the speculation to the reader. Booger would have been proud.

When finished, I sent the story to every newspaper I could think of. Then I waited and waited and waited. There were no offers. Maybe Booger was right. Nobody was interested in two boys from the Ozarks that found themselves on the wrong side of hill justice.

Finally, in desperation, I went to my college newspaper. It took some talking, but I was able to convince the editor to publish it. I can only think now that it must have been a slow week for news articles. The paper printed the article in its entirety, four entire pages that took up the center of that week's newspaper.

I was so proud when it was published. It was my first, and as it turned out, my only attempt at investigative reporting. The story was factual, honest, and void of speculation. It also reached no conclusion, which, as I learned from feedback after the article was published, left readers feeling a little unfulfilled. My ending had eluded me after all. Newspapers, I've been told, like stories that are wrapped up in a bow.

The highlight of my effort, I thought at the time, was when I received a call from a political science professor at my school in St. Joseph. His class had spent an entire period discussing my article. He wanted to meet with me.

I was so excited. Students were talking about my story, political science majors even. I thought they might have some ideas about where I could take the article next, maybe even someone I could contact that might pursue the investigation. I really thought that the professor had summoned me to his office to provide me insight on where I could take the story next.

The young are full of dreams of tomorrow, I suppose.

I remember the professor asking me one question—a question Booger would have cried laughing about: "What makes you think anyone around here cares about some crime in the Ozarks?"

Booger had tried to tell me that no one would care. Yeah, he would find that amusing.

And maybe that's why Booger had spent so much time with me in Joe's Diner after all, why he had gone into great detail about everything that happened to those boys. It was because he was so invested in the story that he couldn't let it go, that it haunted him at night. He needed an outlet. He needed to share with someone, someone that would need to be nearly as vested in it as he was.

The memories of Booger McLain, the Raymonds and the sight of those two boys floating on the surface of Lake Honor would eventually fade. But they never completely disappeared. From time to time, I'd be haunted by those memories in quiet moments or giant storms.

I never saw Booger again, but I did hear from him once, about two years after our meeting. He called me out of the blue. I was married then and had moved twice. How he found me, I wasn't sure. But one day, the phone rang.

"Kid, this is Booger. How the hell are you?"

"Fine, how'd you find me?"

"I'm a Private I. It's kinda my job. What the hell are you doing in Liberty, Kansas? I didn't think anyone went to a place like that on purpose. Did you take a wrong turn somewhere between civilization and the cemetery?"

I was working for a newspaper, doing advertising.

"It's a long story, and this call is probably costing you a fortune."

"I'll bill you," Booger said with a laugh. "I thought I'd get you up-to-date on what's happened since you left."

"Good news, I hope," I responded.

"No, not really. But it's news. Earl Raymond died. His funeral is in two days. Thought you might want to send flowers."

"Shit, what happened to him?"

"His body just shut down. I guess he just got tired of living."

"How's Dorothy doing?"

"As well as you can expect, I guess. She's a strong lady. "There's something else I wanted to tell you, too," he said. "Dorothy hired another private investigator, an ex-cop out of St. Louis. I guess she thought someone from the city might have better success bringing her son's murders to justice."

"Did he?" I asked.

"Don't know. They found his body at the bottom of the mountain off Highway 110. His car was totaled. So was he."

"Damn."

"You can say that again."

"So, is that the end of it?"

"Probably not if Dorothy has her way. But she's going to have a hell of a time getting anyone to investigate her son's death now."

"Booger, do you have an idea why those two boys' bodies were dumped in Lake Honor?"

"I think you know the answer to that."

"No, I don't, Booger. Not really."

"I'm not going to connect the dots for you, son. And, even if I did, it's speculation."

"Booger, I want to ask you something."

"Yeah, kid, what is it?"

"Were you afraid? Was that why you stopped investigating those deaths?"

"Son, whoever said that I stopped?" he said just before hanging up.

I never spoke to him again.

All stories must have an ending. That's what brought me back to S of O over forty years after the death of those boys. When they contacted me on Facebook, Erin and Charlie had brought things to the surface that I couldn't ignore. After thinking about them for some time, I woke up one morning and suddenly knew what I needed to do. I need to go back. I needed to visit S of O again. I needed to go to Lake Honor.

And here I am. Decades later, sitting on the same bench where I spent so much time on during the fall of '73. Five feet from the edge of the pond, fifty feet from the fountain in the shadow of the steeple where those boys' bodies were discovered.

I fell in love for the first time on the shores of Lake Honor. I went here after my father passed away to mourn, to come to terms with his death. I went here on warm late summer and early fall afternoons to study. I went here when I was happy, when I was sad, when I was lost and when I needed answers. I cried. I laughed here. This lake represented some of the happiest times of my youth as well as some of the saddest.

This lake was magical to me—a spiritual realm to itself, somehow separate from the college. Memories made there were timeless. It was my church, my place of reflection. A place where the Earth. Heaven and Hell all met.

Yes, a place of contradictions just like everything I had known and everyone I had met in the Ozarks.

There was darkness in its waters, but there was sunlight reflecting off of it, too. The waters were often calm but, at other times, quite turbulent. The white rays of water jetting up from the fountain were peaceful at times, gently falling back to the surface, creating soft, gentle ripples that flowed toward its banks. But, during storms, the water sprays were erratic, hurling down to punish the surface, creating choppy waves within waves.

It was a place of nature, an artificial pond on a hill.

Sitting on its banks, I felt at peace, knowing what I was there to do.

I had lost track of time. It was getting late in the day. The sun was nearly down. A cool breeze was blowing, and clouds were moving in. The calmness of the lake was beginning to change. It was time.

I reached into my pocket and pulled out the picture I'd brought, the one labeled "Emma" that Dorothy had given me so many years before. I had moved a dozen times, but I had always held onto it. I wasn't sure just why. The drawing was faded now. The edges had yellowed.

I carried it to the water's edge. I kneeled down and laid the drawing gently on the surface of the blue water. And, as I watched, the gentle ripples from the fountain swallowed it up beneath the surface. It was part of the lake now. This was the end. It was home.

— THE END —

Alan Brown grew up in the suburbs of Kansas City and graduated from Shawnee Mission East High School in 1973 and Avila University in 1979. Now he lives in a suburb of St. Louis, MO, with my wife and three daughters. He also has four sons that are grown and living outside the home. He enjoys writing about his experiences growing up, examining the fantastical and dark sides of a person's natural fears. All of his books are based on the reality in his life. He is a fan of Alfred Hitchcock. Like his stories, Alan Brown's will conclude with a twist, something he hopes will take the reader by surprise.

Author Brian Brown. I am a husband, father of four, and a former business and political reporter from Springfield, Missouri, currently living and working in the St. Louis area. I've written five books with my father, Alan Brown, and edited a sixth. All our novels involve our fictional detective, Booger McClain, in what we have dubbed our Ozarks' Noir style. I'm also an amateur photographer: @Bbrownspfd on Instagram. More information about our novels is available on our Facebook page (Alan and Brian Brown Write Stuff): https://www.facebook.com/profile.php?id=100064104282706

www.ingramcontent.com/pod-product-compliance
Lightning Source LLC
Chambersburg PA
CBHW022017170626
46808CB00001B/462